# Pointed Roofs

## Dorothy Richardson

# Contents

# POINTED ROOFS

BY

Dorothy Richardson

# CHAPTER I

1

Miriam left the gaslit hall and went slowly upstairs. The March twilight lay upon the landings, but the staircase was almost dark. The top landing was quite dark and silent. There was no one about. It would be quiet in her room. She could sit by the fire and be quiet and think things over until Eve and Harriett came back with the parcels. She would have time to think about the journey and decide what she was going to say to the Fraulein.

Her new Saratoga trunk stood solid and gleaming in the firelight. To-morrow it would be taken away and she would be gone. The room would be altogether Harriett's. It would never have its old look again. She evaded the thought and moved clumsily to the nearest window. The outline of the round bed and the shapes of the may-trees on either side of the bend of the drive were just visible. There was no escape for her thoughts in this direction. The sense of all she was leaving stirred uncontrollably as she stood looking down into the well-known garden.

Out in the road beyond the invisible lime-trees came the rumble of wheels. The gate creaked and the wheels crunched up the drive, slurring and stopping under the dining-room window.

It was the Thursday afternoon piano-organ, the one that was always in tune. It was early to-day.

She drew back from the window as the bass chords began thumping gently in the darkness. It was better that it should come now than later on, at dinnertime. She could get over it alone up here.

She went down the length of the room and knelt by the fireside with one hand on the mantel-shelf so that she could get up noiselessly and be lighting the gas if anyone came in.

The organ was playing "The Wearin' o' the Green."

It had begun that tune during the last term at school, in the summer.  It made her think of rounders in the hot school garden, singing-classes in the large green room, all the class shouting "Gather roses while ye may," hot afternoons in the shady north room, the sound of turning pages, the hum of the garden beyond the sun-blinds, meetings in the sixth form study. . . . Lilla, with her black hair and the specks of bright amber in the brown of her eyes, talking about free-will.

She stirred the fire.  The windows were quite dark.  The flames shot up and shadows darted.

That summer, which still seemed near to her, was going to fade and desert her, leaving nothing behind.  To-morrow it would belong to a world which would go on without her, taking no heed.  There would still be blissful days.  But she would not be in them.

There would be no more silent sunny mornings with all the day ahead and nothing to do and no end anywhere to anything; no more sitting at the open window in the dining-room, reading Lecky and Darwin and bound "Contemporary Reviews" with roses waiting in the garden to be worn in the afternoon, and Eve and Harriett somewhere about, washing blouses or copying waltzes from the library packet. . . no more Harriett looking in at the end of the morning, rushing her off to the new grand piano to play the "Mikado" and the "Holy Family" duets.  The tennis-club would go on, but she would not be there.  It would begin in May.  Again there would be a white twinkling figure coming quickly along the pathway between the rows of holly-hocks every Saturday afternoon.

Why had he come to tea every Sunday--never missing a single Sunday--all the winter?  Why did he say, "Play 'Abide with me,'" "Play 'Abide with me'" yesterday, if he didn't care?  What was the good of being so quiet and saying nothing?  Why didn't he say "Don't go" or "When are you coming back?"  Eve said he looked perfectly miserable.

There was nothing to look forward to now but governessing and old age.  Perhaps Miss Gilkes was right. . . . Get rid of men and muddles and have things just ordinary and be happy.  "Make up your mind to be happy.  You can be *perfectly* happy without anyone to think about. . . ."  Wearing that large cameo brooch--

long, white, flat-fingered hands and that quiet little laugh. . . . The piano-organ had reached its last tune. In the midst of the final flourish of notes the door flew open. Miriam got quickly to her feet and felt for matches.

2

Harriett came in waggling a thin brown paper parcel.

"Did you hear the Intermezzo? What a dim religious! We got your old collars."

Miriam took the parcel and subsided on to the hearthrug, looking with a new curiosity at Harriett's little, round, firelit face, smiling tightly beneath the rim of her hard felt hat and the bright silk bow beneath her chin.

A footstep sounded on the landing and there was a gentle tap on the open door.

"Oh, come in, Eve--bring some matches. Are the collars piquet, Harry?"

"No, they hadn't got piquet, but they're the plain shape you like. You may thank us they didn't send you things with little rujabiba frills."

Eve came slenderly down the room and Miriam saw with relief that her outdoor things were off. As the gas flared up she drew comfort from her scarlet serge dress, and the soft crimson cheek and white brow of the profile raised towards the flaring jet.

"What are things like downstairs?" she said, staring into the fire.

"I don't know," said Eve. She sighed thoughtfully and sank into a carpet chair under the gas bracket. Miriam glanced at her troubled eyes.

"Pater's only just come in. I think things are pretty rotten," declared Harriett from the hearthrug.

"Isn't it ghastly--for all of us?" Miriam felt treacherously outspoken. It was a relief to be going away. She knew that this sense of relief made her able to speak. "It's never knowing that's so awful. Perhaps he'll get some more money presently and things'll go on again. Fancy mother having it always, ever since we were babies."

"Don't, Mim."

"All right. I won't tell you the words he said, how he put it about the difficulty of getting the money for my things."

"*Don't*, Mim."

Miriam's mind went back to the phrase and her mother's agonised face. She felt utterly desolate in the warm room.

"I wish *I'd* got brains," chirped Harriett, poking the fire with the toe of her boot.

"So you have--more than me."

"Oh--reely."

"You know, I *know* girls, that things are as absolutely ghastly this time as they can possibly be and that something must be done. . . . But you know it's perfectly fearful to face that old school when it comes to the point."

"Oh, my dear, it'll be lovely," said Eve; "all new and jolly, and think how you will enjoy those lectures, you'll simply love them."

"It's all very well to say that. You know you'd feel ill with fright."

"It'll be all right--for *you*--once you're there."

Miriam stared into the fire and began to murmur shamefacedly.

"No more all day bezique. . . . No more days in the West End. . . . No more matinees . . . no more exhibitions . . . no more A.B.C. teas . . . no more insane times . . . no more anything."

"What about holidays? You'll enjoy them all the more."

"I shall be staid and governessy."

"You mustn't. You must be frivolous."

Two deeply-burrowing dimples fastened the clean skin tightly over the bulge of Miriam's smile.

"And marry a German professor," she intoned blithely.

"Don't--don't for *goodney* say that before mother, Miriam."

"D'you mean she minds me going?"

"My *dear!*"

Why did Eve use her cross voice?--stupid . . . "for goodness' sake," not "for goodney." Silly of Eve to talk slang. . . .

"All right. I won't."

"Won't marry a German professor, or won't tell mother, do you mean? . . . Oo--Crumbs! My old cake in the oven!" Harriett hopped to the door.

"Funny Harriett taking to cookery.  It doesn't seem a bit like her."

"She'll have to do something--so shall I, I s'pose."

"It seems awful."

"We shall simply have to."

"It's awful," said Miriam, shivering.

"Poor old girl.  I expect you feel horrid because you're tired with all the packing and excitement."

"Oh well, anyhow, it's simply ghastly."

"You'll feel better to-morrow."

"D'you think I shall?"

"Yes--you're so strong," said Eve, flushing and examining her nails.

"How d'you mean?"

"Oh--all sorts of ways."

"What way?"

"Oh--well--you arranging all this--I mean answering the advertisement and settling it all."

"Oh well, you know you backed me up."

"Oh yes, but other things. . . ."

"What?"

"Oh, I was thinking about you having no religion."

"Oh."

"You must have such splendid principles to keep you straight," said Eve, and cleared her throat, "I mean, you must have such a lot in you."

"Me?"

"Yes, of course."

"I don't know where it comes in.  What have I done?"

"Oh, well, it isn't so much what you've done--you have such a good time. . . . Everybody admires you and all that . . . you know what I mean--you're so clever. . . . You're always in the right."

"That's just what everybody hates!"

"Well, my dear, I wish I had your mind."

"You needn't," said Miriam.

"You're all right--you'll come out all right.  You're one of those strong-minded people who have to go through a period of doubt."

"But, my *dear*," said Miriam grateful and proud, "I feel such a humbug. You know when I wrote that letter to the Fraulein I said I was a member of the Church. I know what it will be, I shall have to take the English girls to church."

"Oh, well, you won't mind that."

"It will make me simply ill--I could *never* describe to you," said Miriam, with her face aglow, "what it is to me to hear some silly man drone away with an undistributed middle term."

"They're not all like that."

"Oh, well, then it will be ignoratio elenchi or argumentum ad hominem--"

"Oh, yes, but they're not the *service*."

"The service I can't make head or tail of--think of the Athanasian."

"Yes." Eve stirred uneasily and began to execute a gentle scale with her tiny tightly-knit blue and white hand upon her knee.

"It'll be ghastly," continued Miriam, "not having anyone to pour out to--I've told you such a lot these last few days."

"Yes, hasn't it been funny? I seem to know you all at once so much better."

"Well--don't you think I'm perfectly hateful?"

"No. I admire you more than ever. I think you're simply splendid."

"Then you simply don't know me."

"Yes I do. And you'll be able to write to me."

Eve, easily weeping, hugged her and whispered, "You mustn't. I can't see you break down--don't--don't--don't. We can't be blue your last night. . . . Think of nice things. . . . There *will* be nice things again . . . there will, will, will, *will*."

Miriam pursed her lips to a tight bunch and sat twisting her long thickish fingers. Eve stood up in her tears. Her smile and the curves of her mouth were unchanged by her weeping, and the crimson had spread and deepened a little in the long oval of her face. Miriam watched the changing crimson. Her eyes went to and fro between it and the neatly pinned masses of brown hair.

"I'm going to get some hot water," said Eve, "and we'll make ourselves glorious."

Miriam watched her as she went down the long room--the great oval of dark hair, the narrow neck, the narrow back, tight, plump little hands hanging in profile, white, with a purple pad near the wrist.

3

When Miriam woke the next morning she lay still with closed eyes. She had dreamed that she had been standing in a room in the German school and the staff had crowded round her, looking at her. They had dreadful eyes--eyes like the eyes of hostesses she remembered, eyes she had seen in trains and 'buses, eyes from the old school. They came and stood and looked at her, and saw her as she was, without courage, without funds or good clothes or beauty, without charm or interest, without even the skill to play a part. They looked at her with loathing. "Board and lodging--privilege to attend Masters' lectures and laundry (body-linen only)." That was all she had thought of and clutched at--all along, since first she read the Fraulein's letter. Her keep and the chance of learning . . . and Germany--Germany, das deutsche Vaterland--Germany, all woods and mountains and tenderness--Hermann and Dorothea in the dusk of a happy village.

And it would really be those women, expecting things of her. They would be so affable at first. She had been through it a million times--all her life--all eternity. They would smile those hateful women's smiles--smirks--self-satisfied smiles as if everybody were agreed about everything. She loathed women. They always smiled. All the teachers had at school, all the girls, but Lilla. Eve did . . . maddeningly sometimes . . . Mother . . . it was the only funny horrid thing about her. Harriett didn't. . . . Harriett laughed. She was strong and hard somehow. . . .

Pater knew how hateful all the world of women were and despised them.

He never included her with them; or only sometimes when she pretended, or he didn't understand. . . .

Someone was saying "Hi!" a gurgling muffled shout, a long way off.

She opened her eyes. It was bright morning. She saw the twist of Harriett's body lying across the edge of the bed. With a gasp she flung herself over her own side. Harry, old Harry, jolly old Harry had remembered the Grand Ceremonial. In a moment her own head hung, her long hair flinging back on to the floor, her eyes gazing across the bed at the reversed snub of Harriett's face. It was flushed in the midst of the wiry hair which stuck out all round it but did not reach the floor. "Hi!"

they gurgled solemnly, "Hi. . . . Hi!" shaking their heads from side to side. Then their four frilled hands came down and they flumped out of the high bed.

They performed an uproarious toilet. It seemed so safe up there in the bright bare room. Miriam's luggage had been removed. It was away somewhere in the house; far away and unreal and unfelt as her parents somewhere downstairs, and the servants away in the basement getting breakfast and Sarah and Eve always incredible, getting quietly up in the next room. Nothing was real but getting up with old Harriett in this old room.

She revelled in Harriett's delicate buffoonery ("voluntary incongruity" she quoted to herself as she watched her)--the titles of some of the books on Harriett's shelf, "Ungava; a Tale of the North," "Grimm's Fairy Tales," "John Halifax," "Swiss Family Robinson" made her laugh. The curtained recesses of the long room stretched away into space.

She went about dimpling and responding, singing and masquerading as her large hands did their work.

She intoned the titles on her own shelf--as a response to the quiet swearing and jesting accompanying Harriett's occupations. "The Voyage of the Beeeeeeagle," she sang "Scott's Poetical *Works*." Villette--Longfellow--Holy Bible *with* Apocrypha--Egmont--

"Binks!" squealed Harriett daintily. "Yink grink binks."

"Books!" she responded in a low tone, and flushed as if she had given Harriett an affectionate hug. "My rotten books. . . ." She would come back, and read all her books more carefully. She had packed some. She could not remember which and why.

"Binks," she said, and it was quite easy for them to crowd together at the little dressing-table. Harriett was standing in her little faded red moirette petticoat and a blue flannelette dressing-jacket brushing her wiry hair. Miriam reflected that she need no longer hate her for the set of her clothes round her hips. She caught sight of her own faded jersey and stiff, shapeless black petticoat in the mirror. Harriett's "Hinde's" lay on the dressing-table, her own still lifted the skin of her forehead in suffused puckerings against the shank of each pin.

Unperceived, she eyed the tiny stiff plait of hair which stuck out almost horizontally from the nape of Harriett's neck, and watched her combing out the tightly-curled fringe standing stubbily out along her forehead and extending like a thickset hedge midway across the crown of her head, where it stopped abruptly against the sleekly-brushed longer strands which strained over her poll and disappeared into the plait.

"Your old wool'll be just right in Germany," remarked Harriett.

"Mm."

"You ought to do it in basket plaits like Sarah."

"I wish I could.  I can't think how she does it."

"Ike spect it's easy enough."

"Mm."

"But you're all right, anyhow."

"Anyhow, it's no good bothering when you're plain."

"You're *not* plain."

Miriam looked sharply round.

"Go on, Gooby."

"You're not.  You don't know.  Granny said you'll be a bonny woman, and Sarah thinks you've got the best shape face and the best complexion of any of us, and cook was simply crying her eyes out last night and said you were the light of the house with your happy, pretty face, and mother said you're much too attractive to go about alone, and that's partly why Pater's going with you to Hanover, silly. . . . You're not plain," she gasped.

Miriam's amazement silenced her.  She stood back from the mirror.  She could not look into it until Harriett had gone.  The phrases she had just heard rang in her head without meaning.  But she knew she would remember all of them.  She went on doing her hair with downcast eyes.  She had seen Harriett vividly, and had longed to crush her in her arms and kiss her little round cheeks and the snub of her nose.  Then she wanted her to be gone.

Presently Harriett took up a brooch and skated down the room, "Ta-ra-ra-la-eee-tee!" she carolled, "don't be long," and disappeared.

"I'm pretty," murmured Miriam, planting herself in front of the dressing-table.  "I'm pretty--they like me--they *like* me.  Why didn't I know?"  She did not look into the mirror.  "They all like me, *me*."

The sound of the breakfast-bell came clanging up through the house.  She hurried to her side of the curtained recess. Hanging there were her old red stockinette jersey and her blue skirt . . . never again . . . just once more . . . she could change afterwards. Her brown, heavy best dress with puffed and gauged sleeves and thick gauged and gathered boned bodice was in her hand. She hung it once more on its peg and quickly put on her old things. The jersey was shiny with wear. "You darling old things," she muttered as her arms slipped down the sleeves.

The door of the next room opened quietly and she heard Sarah and Eve go decorously downstairs. She waited until their footsteps had died away and then went very slowly down the first flight, fastening her belt. She stopped at the landing window, tucking the frayed end of the petersham under the frame of the buckle . . . they were all downstairs, liking her. She could not face them. She was too excited and too shy. . . . She had never once thought of their "feeling" her going away . . . saying goodbye to each one . . . all minding and sorry--even the servants. She glanced fearfully out into the garden, seeing nothing. Someone called up from the breakfast-room doorway, "Mim--my!" How surprised Mr. Bart had been when he discovered that they themselves never knew whose voice it was of all four of them unless you saw the person, "but yours is really richer" . . . it was cheek to say that.

"Mimm--my!"

Suddenly she longed to be gone--to have it all over and be gone.

She heard the kak-kak of Harriett's wooden heeled slippers across the tiled hall. She glanced down the well of the staircase. Harriett was mightily swinging the bell, scattering a little spray of notes at each end of her swing.

With a frightened face Miriam crept back up the stairs. Violently slamming the bedroom door, "I'm a-comin'--I'm a-comin'," she shouted and ran downstairs.

## CHAPTER II

### 1

The crossing was over. They were arriving. The movement of the little steamer that had collected the passengers from the packet-boat drove the raw air against Miriam's face. In her tired brain the grey river and the flat misty shores slid constantly into a vision of the gaslit dining-room at home . . . the large clear glowing fire, the sounds of the family voices. Every effort to obliterate the picture brought back again the moment that had come at the dinner-table as they all sat silent for an instant with downcast eyes and she had suddenly longed to go on for ever just sitting there with them all.

Now, in the boat she wanted to be free for the strange grey river and the grey shores. But the home scenes recurred relentlessly. Again and again she went through the last moments . . . the goodbyes, the unexpected convulsive force of her mother's arms, her own dreadful inability to give any answering embrace. She could not remember saying a single word. There had been a feeling that came like a tide carrying her away. Eager and dumb and remorseful she had gone out of the house and into the cab with Sarah, and then had come the long sitting in the loop-line train . . . "talk about something" . . . Sarah sitting opposite and her unchanged voice saying "What shall we talk about?" And then a long waiting, and the brown leather strap swinging against the yellow grained door, the smell of dust and the dirty wooden flooring, with the noise of the wheels underneath going to the swinging tune of one of Heller's "Sleepless Nights." The train had made her sway with its movements. How still Sarah seemed to sit, fixed in the old life. Nothing had come but strange cruel emotions.

After the suburban train nothing was distinct until the warm snowflakes were drifting against her face through the cold darkness on Harwich quay.  Then, after what seemed like a great loop of time spent going helplessly up a gangway towards "the world" she had stood, face to face with the pale polite stewardess in her cabin.  "I had better have a lemon, cut in two," she had said, feeling suddenly stifled with fear.  For hours she had lain despairing, watching the slowly swaying walls of her cabin or sinking with closed eyes through invertebrate dipping spaces.  Before each releasing paroxysm she told herself "this is like death; one day I shall die, it will be like this."

She supposed there would be breakfast soon on shore, a firm room and a teapot and cups and saucers.  Cold and exhaustion would come to an end.  She would be talking to her father.

2

He was standing near her with the Dutchman who had helped her off the boat and looked after her luggage.  The Dutchman was listening, deferentially.  Miriam saw the strong dark blue beam of his eyes.

"Very good, very good," she heard him say, "fine education in German schools."

Both men were smoking cigars.

She wanted to draw herself upright and shake out her clothes.

"Select," she heard, "excellent staff of masters . . . daughters of gentlemen."

"Pater is trying to make the Dutchman think I am being taken as a pupil to a finishing school in Germany."  She thought of her lonely pilgrimage to the West End agency, of her humiliating interview, of her heart-sinking acceptance of the post, the excitements and misgivings she had had, of her sudden challenge of them all that evening after dinner, and their dismay and remonstrance and reproaches-- of her fear and determination in insisting and carrying her point and making them begin to be interested in her plan.

But she shared her father's satisfaction in impressing the Dutchman.  She knew that she was at one with him in that.  She glanced at him.  There could be no doubt that he was playing the rôle of the English gentleman.  Poor dear.  It was what he had always wanted to be.  He had sacrificed everything to the idea of being a "person of leisure and cultivation." Well, after all, it was true in a way. He was--and he had, she knew, always wanted her to be the same and she *was* going to finish her education abroad . . . in Germany. . . . They were nearing a little low quay backed by a tremendous saffron-coloured hoarding announcing in black letters "Sunlight Zeep."

3

"Did you see, Pater; did you *see?*"

They were walking rapidly along the quay.

"Did you see? Sunlight *Zeep!*"

She listened to his slightly scuffling stride at her side.

Glancing up she saw his face excited and important. He was not listening. He was being an English gentleman, "emerging" from the Dutch railway station.

"Sunlight *Zeep*," she shouted. "*Zeep*, Pater!"

He glanced down at her and smiled condescendingly.

"Ah, yes," he admitted with a laugh.

There were Dutch faces for Miriam--men, women and children coming towards her with sturdy gait.

"They're talking Dutch! They're all talking *Dutch!*"

The foreign voices, the echoes in the little narrow street, the flat waterside effect of the sounds, the bright clearness she had read of, brought tears to her eyes.

"The others *must* come here," she told herself, pitying them all.

They had an English breakfast at the Victoria Hotel and went out and hurried about the little streets. They bought cigars and rode through the town on a little tramway. Presently they were in a train watching the Dutch landscape go by. One level stretch succeeded another. Miriam wanted to go out alone under the grey sky and walk over the flat fields shut in by poplars.

She looked at the dykes and the windmills with indifferent eyes, but her desire for the flat meadows grew.

Late at night, seated wide-awake opposite her sleeping companion, rushing towards the German city, she began to think.

4

It was a fool's errand. . . . To undertake to go to the German school and teach . . . to be going there . . . with nothing to give. The moment would come when there would be a class sitting round a table waiting for her to speak. She imagined one of the rooms at the old school, full of scornful girls. . . . How was English taught? How did you begin? English grammar . . . in German? Her heart beat in her throat. She had never thought of that . . . the rules of English grammar? Parsing and analysis. . . . Anglo-Saxon prefixes and suffixes . . . gerundial infinitive. . . . It was too late to look anything up. Perhaps there would be a class to-morrow. . . . The German lessons at school had been dreadfully good. . . . Fraulein's grave face . . . her perfect knowledge of every rule . . . her clear explanations in English . . . her examples. . . . All these things were there, in English grammar. . . . And she had undertaken to teach them and could not even speak German.

Monsieur . . . had talked French all the time . . . dictees . . . lectures . . . Le Conscrit . . . Waterloo . . . La Maison Deserte . . . his careful voice reading on and on . . . until the room disappeared. . . . She must do that for her German girls. Read English to them and make them happy. . . . But first there must be verbs . . . there had been cahiers of them . . . first, second, third conjugation. . . . It was impudence, an impudent invasion . . . the dreadful clever, foreign school. . . . They would laugh at her. . . . She began to repeat the English alphabet. . . . She doubted whether, faced with a class, she could reach the end without a mistake. . . . She reached Z and went on to the parts of speech.

5

There would be a moment when she must have an explanation with the Fraulein. Perhaps she could tell her that she found the teaching was beyond her scope and then find a place somewhere as a servant. She remembered things she had heard about German servants--that whenever they even dusted a room they cleaned the windows and on Sundays they waited at lunch in muslin dresses and afterwards went to balls. She feared even the German servants would despise her. They had

never been allowed into the kitchen at home except when there was jam-making .
. . she had never made a bed in her life. . . . A shop? But that would mean knowing
German and being quick at giving change. Impossible. Perhaps she could find some
English people in Hanover who would help her. There was an English colony she
knew, and an English church. But that would be like going back. That must not
happen. She would rather stay abroad on any terms--away from England--English
people. She had scented something, a sort of confidence, everywhere, in her hours
in Holland, the brisk manner of the German railway officials and the serene assurance of the travelling Germans she had seen, confirmed her impression. Away out
here, the sense of imminent catastrophe that had shadowed all her life so far, had
disappeared. Even here in this dim carriage, with disgrace ahead she felt that there
was freedom somewhere at hand. Whatever happened she would hold to that.

6

She glanced up at her small leather handbag lying in the rack and thought of
the solid money in her purse. Twenty-five shillings. It was a large sum and she was
to have more as she needed.

She glanced across at the pale face with its point of reddish beard, the long
white hands laid one upon the other on the crossed knees. He had given her twenty-five shillings and there was her fare and his, and his return fare and her new
trunk and all the things she had needed. It must be the end of taking money from
him. She was grown up. She was the strong-minded one. She must manage. With
a false position ahead and after a short space, disaster, she must get along.

The peaceful Dutch fields came to her mind. They looked so secure. They had
passed by too soon. We have always been in a false position, she pondered. Always
lying and pretending and keeping up a show--never daring to tell anybody. . . . Did
she want to tell anybody? To come out into the open and be helped and have things
arranged for her and do things like other people? No. . . . No. . . . "Miriam always
likes to be different"--"Society is no boon to those not sociable." Dreadful things . .
. and the girls laughing together about them. What did they really mean?

"Society is no boon to those not sociable"--on her birthday-page in Ellen
Sharpe's birthday-book. Ellen handed it to her going upstairs and had chanted the

words out to the others and smiled her smile . . . she had not asked her to write her name . . . was it unsociable to dislike so many of the girls. . . . Ellen's people were in the Indian . . . her thoughts hesitated. . . . Sivvle . . . something grand--All the grand girls were horrid . . . somehow mean and sly . . . Sivvle . . . *Sivvle* . . . *Civil!* Of course! Civil *what?*

Miriam groaned. She was a governess now. Someone would ask her that question. She would ask Pater before he went. . . . No, she would not. . . . If only he would answer a question simply, and not with a superior air as if he had invented the thing he was telling about. She felt she had a right to all the knowledge there was, without fuss . . . oh, without fuss--without fuss and--emotion. . . . I *am* unsociable, I suppose--she mused. She could not think of anyone who did not offend her. I don't like men and I loathe women. I am a misanthrope. So's Pater. He despises women and can't get on with men. We are different--it's us, him and me. He's failed us because he's different and if he weren't we should be like other people. Everything in the railway responded and agreed. Like other people . . . horrible. . . . She thought of the fathers of girls she knew--the Poole girls, for instance, they were to be "independent" trained and certificated--she envied that--but her envy vanished when she remembered how heartily she had agreed when Sarah called them "sharp" and "knowing."

Mr. Poole was a business man . . . common . . . trade. . . . If Pater had kept to Grandpa's business they would be trade, too--well-off, now--all married. Perhaps as it was he had thought they would marry.

### 7

She thought sleepily of her Wesleyan grandparents, gravely reading the "Wesleyan Methodist Recorder," the shop at Babington, her father's discontent, his solitary fishing and reading, his discovery of music . . . science . . . classical music in the first Novello editions . . . Faraday . . . speaking to Faraday after lectures. Marriage . . . the new house . . . the red brick wall at the end of the garden where young peach-trees were planted . . . running up and downstairs and singing . . . both of them singing in the rooms and the garden . . . she sometimes with her hair down and then when visitors were expected pinned in coils under a little cap and wearing a small hoop . . . the garden and lawns and shrubbery and the long kitchen-garden and the summer-house under the oaks beyond and the pretty old gabled "town" on the river and the woods all along the river valley and the hills shining up out of the mist. The snow man they both made in the winter--the birth of Sarah and then Eve . . . his studies and book-buying--and after five years her own disappointing birth as the third girl, and the coming of Harriett just over a year later . . . her mother's illness, money troubles--their two years at the sea to retrieve . . . the disappearance of the sunlit red-walled garden always in full summer sunshine with the sound of bees in it or dark from windows . . . the narrowing of the house-life down to the Marine Villa--with the sea creeping in--wading out through the green shallows, out and out till you were more than waist deep--shrimping and prawning hour after hour for weeks together . . . poking in the rock pools, watching the sun and the colours in the strange afternoons . . . then the sudden large house at Barnes with the "drive" winding to the door. . . . He used to come home from the City and the Constitutional Club and sometimes instead of reading "The Times" or the "Globe" or the "Proceedings of the British Association" or Herbert Spencer, play Pope Joan or Jacoby with them all, or Table Billiards and laugh and be "silly" and take his turn at being "bumped" by Timmy going the round of the long dining-room table, tail in the air; he had taken Sarah and Eve to see "Don Giovanni" and "Winter's Tale" and the new piece, "Lohengrin." No one at the tennis-club had seen that. He had good taste. No one else had been to Madame Schumann's Farewell . . . sitting at the piano with her curtains of hair and her dreamy smile . . . and the Philharmonic Concerts. No one else knew about the lectures at the Royal Institution, beginning at nine on Fridays. . . . No one else's father went with a party of scientific men "for the advancement of science" to Norway or America, seeing the Falls and the Yosemite Valley. No one else took his children as far as Dawlish for the holidays, travelling all day, from eight until seven . . . no esplanade, the old stone jetty and coves and cowrie shells. . . .

# CHAPTER III

## 1

Miriam was practising on the piano in the larger of the two English bed-rooms. Two other pianos were sounding in the house, one across the landing and the other in the saal where Herr Kapellmeister Bossenberger was giving a music-lesson. The rest of the girls were gathered in the large schoolroom under the care of Mademoiselle for Saturday's *raccommodage*. It was the last hour of the week's work. Presently there would be a great gonging, the pianos would cease, Fraulein's voice would sound up through the house "Anziehen zum Aus-geh-hen!"

There would be the walk, dinner, the Saturday afternoon home-letters to be written and then, until Monday, holiday, freedom to read and to talk English and idle. And there was a new arrival in the house. Ulrica Hesse had come. Miriam had seen her. There had been three large leather trunks in the hall and a girl with a smooth pure oval of pale face standing wrapped in dark furs, gazing about her with eyes for which Miriam had no word, liquid--limpid--great-saucers, no--pools . . . great round deeps. . . . She had felt about for something to express them as she went upstairs with her roll of music. Fraulein Pfaff who had seemed to hover and smile about the girl as if half afraid to speak to her, had put out a hand for Miriam and said almost deprecatingly, "Ach, mm, dies' ist unser Ulrica."

The girl's thin fingers had come out of her furs and fastened convulsively--like cold, throbbing claws on to the breadth of Miriam's hand.

"Unsere englische Lehrerin--our teacher from England," smiled Fraulein.

"Lehrerin!" breathed the girl. Something flinched behind her great eyes. The fingers relaxed, and Miriam feeling within her a beginning of response, had gone upstairs.

As she reached the upper landing she began to distinguish against the clangour of chromatic passages assailing the house from the echoing saal, the gentle tones of the nearer piano, the one in the larger German bedroom opposite the front room for which she was bound.  She paused for a moment at the top of the stairs and listened.  A little swaying melody came out to her, muted by the closed door.  Her grasp on the roll of music slackened.  A radiance came for a moment behind the gravity of her face.  Then the careful unstumbling repetition of a difficult passage drew her attention to the performer, her arms dropped to her sides and she passed on.  It was little Bergmann, the youngest girl in the school.  Her playing, on the bad old piano in the dark dressing-room in the basement, had prepared Miriam for the difference between the performance of these German girls and nearly all the piano-playing she had heard.  It was the morning after her arrival.  She had been unpacking and had taken, on the advice of Mademoiselle, her heavy boots and outdoor things down to the basement room.  She had opened the door on Emma sitting at the piano in her blue and buff check ribbon-knotted stuff dress.  Miriam had expected her to turn her head and stop playing.  But as, arms full, she closed the door with her shoulders, the child's profile remained unconcerned.  She noticed the firmly-poised head, the thick creamy neck that seemed bare with its absence of collar-band and the soft frill of tucker stitched right on to the dress, the thick cable of string-coloured hair reaching just beyond the rim of the leather-covered music stool, the steel-headed points of the little slippers gleaming as they worked the pedals, the serene eyes steadily following the music.  She played on and Miriam recognised a quality she had only heard occasionally at concerts, and in the playing of one of the music teachers at school.

She had stood amazed, pretending to he fumbling for empty pegs as this round-faced child of fourteen went her way to the end of her page.  Then Miriam had ventured to interrupt and to ask her about the hanging arrangements, and the child had risen and speaking soft South German had suggested and poked tip-toeing about amongst the thickly-hung garments and shown a motherly solicitude over the disposal of Miriam's things.  Miriam noted the easy range of the child's voice, how smoothly it slid from birdlike queries and chirpings, to the consoling tones of the lower register.  It seemed to leave undisturbed the softly-rounded, faintly-mottled chin and cheeks and the full unpouting lips that lay quietly one upon the other be-fore she spoke, and opened flexibly but somehow hardly moved to her speech and afterwards closed again gradually until they lay softly blossoming as before.

Emma had gathered up her music when the clothes were arranged, sighing and lamenting gently, "Ware ich nur zu Hause"--how happy one was at home--her little voice filled with tears and her cheeks flushed, "haypie, haypie to home," she complained as she slid her music into its case, "where all so good, so nice, so beauti-ful," and they had gone, side by side, up the dark uncarpeted stone stairs leading from the basement to the hall. Half-way up, Emma had given Miriam a shy firm hug and then gone decorously up the remainder of the flight.

The sense of that sudden little embrace recurred often to Miriam during the course of the first day.

It was unlike any contact she had known--more motherly than her mother's. Neither of her sisters could have embraced her like that. She did not know that a human form could bring such a sense of warm nearness, that human contours could be eloquent--or anyone so sweetly daring.

2

That first evening at Waldstrasse there had been a performance that had com-pleted the transformation of Miriam's English ideas of "music." She had caught the word "Vorspielen" being bandied about the long tea-table, and had gathered that there was to be an informal playing of "pieces" before Fraulein Pfaff. She welcomed the event. It relieved her from the burden of being in high focus--the relief had come as soon as she took her place at the gaslit table. No eye seemed to notice her. The English girls having sat out two meal-times with her, had ceased the hard-eyed observation which had made the long silence of the earlier repasts only less embarrassing than Fraulein's questions about England. The four Germans who had neither stared nor even appeared aware of her existence, talked cheerfully across the table in a general exchange that included tall Fraulein Pfaff smiling her horse-smile--Miriam provisionally called it--behind the tea-urn, as chairman. The six English-speaking girls, grouped as it were towards their chief, a dark-skinned, athletic looking Australian with hot, brown, slightly blood-shot eyes sitting as vice-president opposite Fraulein, joined occasionally, in solo and chorus, and Miriam noted with relief a unanimous atrocity of accent in their enviable fluency. Rapid *sotto voce* commentary and half-suppressed wordless by-play located still more clearly the English quarter. Animation flowed and flowed. Miriam safely ignored, scarcely heeding, but warmed and almost happy, basked. She munched her black bread and butter, liberally smeared with the rich savoury paste of liver sausage, and drank her sweet weak tea and knew that she was very tired, sleepy and tired. She glanced, from her place next to Emma Bergmann and on Fraulein's left hand, down the table to where Mademoiselle sat next the Martins in similar relation to the vice-president. Mademoiselle, preceding her up through the quiet house carrying the jugs of hot water, had been her first impression on her arrival the previous night. She had turned when they reached the candle-lit attic with its high uncurtained windows and red-covered box beds, and standing on the one strip of matting in her full-skirted grey wincey dress with its neat triple row of black ribbon velvet near the hem, had shown Miriam steel-blue eyes smiling from a little triangular sprite-like face under a high-standing pouf of soft dark hair, and said, "Voila!" Miriam had never imagined anything in the least like her. She had said, "Oh, thank you," and taken the jug and had hurriedly and silently got to bed, weighed down by wonders. They had begun to talk in the dark. Miriam had reaped sweet comfort in learning that this seemingly unreal creature who was, she soon perceived, not educated-- as she understood education--was the resident French governess, was seventeen years old and a Protestant. Such close quarters with a French girl was bewildering enough--had she been a Roman Catholic, Miriam felt she could not have endured her proximity. She was evidently a special kind of French girl--a Protestant from East France--Besan on--Besan on--Miriam had tried the pretty word over until unexpectedly she had fallen asleep.

They had risen hurriedly in the cold March gloom and Miriam had not spoken to her since. There she sat, dainty and quiet and fresh. White frillings shone now at the neck and sleeves of her little grey dress. She looked a clean and clear miniature against the general dauby effect of the English girls--poor though, Miriam was sure; perhaps as poor as she. She felt glad as she watched her gentle sprite-like wistfulness that she would be upstairs in that great bare attic again to-night. In repose her face looked pinched. There was something about the nose and mouth--Miriam mused . . . *frugal*--John Gilpin's wife--how sleepy she was.

3

The conversation was growing boisterous. She took courage to raise her head towards the range of girls opposite to her. Those quite near to her she could not scrutinise. Some influence coming to her from these German girls prevented her risking with them any meeting of the eyes that was not brought about by direct speech. But she felt them. She felt Emma Bergmann's warm plump presence close at her side and liked to take food handed by her. She was conscious of the pink bulb of Minna Blum's nose shining just opposite to her, and of the way the light caught the blond sheen of her exquisitely coiled hair as she turned her always smiling face and responded to the louder remarks with, "Oh, thou *dear* God!" or "Is it possible!" "How charming, *charming*," or "What in life dost thou say, rascal!"

Next to her was the faint glare of Elsa Speier's silent sallowness. Her clear-threaded nimbus of pallid hair was the lowest point in the range of figures across the table. She darted quick glances at one and another without moving her head, and Miriam felt that her pale eyes fully met would be cunning and malicious.

After Elsa the "English" began with Judy. Miriam guessed when she heard her ask for Brodchen that she was Scotch. She sat slightly askew and ate eagerly, stooping over her plate with smiling mouth and downcast heavily-freckled face. Unless spoken to she did not speak, but she laughed often, a harsh involuntary laugh immediately followed by a drowning flush. When she was not flushed her eyelashes shone bright black against the unstained white above her cheek-bones. She had coarse fuzzy red-brown hair.

Miriam decided that she was negligible.

Next to Judy were the Martins. They were as English as they could be. She felt she must have noticed them a good deal at breakfast and dinner-time without knowing it. Her eyes after one glance at the claret-coloured merino dresses with hard white collars and cuffs, came back to her plate as from a familiar picture. She still saw them sitting very upright, side by side, with the front strands of their hair strained smoothly back, tied just on the crest of the head with brown ribbon and going down in "rats'-tails" to join the rest of their hair which hung straight and flat half-way down their backs. The elder was dark with thick shoulders and heavy features. Her large expressionless rich brown eyes flashed slowly and reflected the light. They gave Miriam a slight feeling of nausea. She felt she knew what her hands were like without looking at them. The younger was thin and pale and slightly hollow-cheeked. She had pale eyes, cold, like a fish, thought Miriam. They both had deep hollow voices.

When she glanced again they were watching the Australian with their four strange eyes and laughing German phrases at her, "Go on, Gertrude!" "Are you *sure,* Gertrude?" "How do you *know!*"

Miriam had not yet dared to glance in the direction of the Australian. Her eyes at dinner-time had cut like sharp steel. Turning, however, towards the danger zone, without risking the coming of its presiding genius within the focus of her glasses she caught a glimpse of "Jimmie" sitting back in her chair tall and plump and neat, and shaking with wide-mouthed giggles. Miriam wondered at the high peak of hair on the top of her head and stared at her pearly little teeth. There was something funny about her mouth. Even when she strained it wide it was narrow and tiny--rabbity. She raised a short arm and began patting her peak of hair with a tiny hand which showed a small onyx seal ring on the little finger. "Ask Judy!" she giggled, in a fruity squeak.

"Ask Judy!" they all chorused, laughing.

Judy cast an appealing flash of her eyes sideways at nothing, flushed furiously and mumbled, "Ik weiss nik--I don't know."

In the outcries and laughter which followed, Miriam noticed only the hoarse hacking laugh of the Australian. Her eyes flew up the table and fixed her as she sat laughing, her chair drawn back, her knees crossed--tea was drawing to an end. The detail of her terrifyingly stylish ruddy-brown frieze dress with its Norfolk jacket bodice and its shiny black leather belt was hardly distinguishable from the dark background made by the folding doors. But the dreadful outline of her shoulders was visible, the squarish oval of her face shone out--the wide forehead from which the wiry black hair was combed to a high puff, the red eyes, black now, the long straight nose, the wide laughing mouth with the enormous teeth.

Her voice conquered easily.

"Nein," she tromboned, through the din.

Mademoiselle's little finger stuck up sharply like a steeple, her mouth said, "Oh--Oh----"

Fraulein's smile was at its widest, waiting the issue.

"Nein," triumphed the Australian, causing a lull.

"Leise, Kinder, leise, doucement, gentlay," chided Fraulein, still smiling.

"Hermann, *yes,*" proceeded the Australian, "aber Hugo-- *ne!*"

Miriam heard it agreed in the end that someone named Hugo did not wear a moustache, though someone named Hermann did. She was vaguely shocked and interested.

4

After tea the great doors were thrown open and the girls filed into the saal. It was a large high room furnished like a drawing-room--enough settees and easy chairs to accommodate more than all the girls. The polished floor was uncarpeted save for an archipelago of mats and rugs in the wide circle of light thrown by the four-armed chandelier. A grand piano was pushed against the wall in the far corner of the room, between the farthest of the three high French windows and the shining pillar of porcelain stove.

5

The high room, the bright light, the plentiful mirrors, the long sweep of lace curtains, the many faces--the girls seemed so much more numerous scattered here than they had when collected in the schoolroom--brought Miriam the sense of the misery of social occasions. She wondered whether the girls were nervous. She was glad that music lessons were no part of her remuneration. She thought of dreadful experiences of playing before people. The very first time, at home, when she had played a duet with Eve--Eve playing a little running melody in the treble--her own part a page of minims. The minims had swollen until she could not see whether they were lines or spaces, and her fingers had been so weak after the first unexpectedly loud note that she could hardly make any sound. Eve had said "louder" and her fingers had suddenly stiffened and she had worked them from her elbows like

sticks at the end of her trembling wrists and hands. Eve had noticed her dreadful movements and resented being elbowed. She had heard nothing then but her
hard loud minims till the end, and then as she stood dizzily up someone had said
she had a nice firm touch, and she had pushed her angry way from the piano across
the hearthrug. She should always remember the clear red-hot mass of the fire and
the bottle of green Chartreuse warming on the blue and cream tiles. There were
probably only two or three guests, but the room had seemed full of people, stupid
people who had made her play. How angry she had been with Eve for noticing her
discomfiture and with the forgotten guest for her silly remark. She knew she had
simply poked the piano. Then there had been the annual school concert, all the
girls almost unrecognisable with fear. She had learnt her pieces by heart for those
occasions and played them through with trembling limbs and burning eyes--alter-
nately thumping with stiff fingers and feeling her whole hand faint from the wrist
on to the notes which fumbled and slurred into each other almost soundlessly until
the thumping began again. At the musical evenings, organised by Eve as a winter
set-off to the tennis-club, she had both played and sung, hoping each time afresh to
be able to reproduce the effects which came so easily when she was alone or only
with Eve. But she could not discover the secret of getting rid of her nervousness.
Only twice had she succeeded--at the last school concert when she had been too
miserable to be nervous and Mr. Strood had told her she did him credit and, once
she had sung "Chanson de Florian" in a way that had astonished her own listening
ear--the notes had laughed and thrilled out into the air and come back to her from
the wall behind the piano. . . . The day before the tennis tournament.

6

The girls were all settling down to fancy work, the white-cuffed hands of the
Martins were already jerking crochet needles, faces were bending over fine embroideries and Minna Blum had trundled a mounted lace-pillow into the brighter
light.

Miriam went to the schoolroom and fetched from her work-basket the piece
of canvas partly covered with red and black wool in diamond pattern that was her
utmost experience of fancy work.

As she returned she half saw Fraulein Pfaff, sitting as if enthroned on a high-backed chair in front of the centremost of the mirrors filling the wall spaces between the long French windows, signal to her, to come to that side of the room.

Timorously ignoring the signal she got herself into a little low chair in the shadow of the half-closed swing door and was spreading out her wool-work on her knee when the Vorspielen began.

Emma Bergmann was playing.  The single notes of the opening *motif* of Chopin's Fifteenth Nocturne fell pensively into the waiting room.  Miriam, her fatigue forgotten, slid to a featureless freedom.  It seemed to her that the light with which the room was filled grew brighter and clearer.  She felt that she was looking at nothing and yet was aware of the whole room like a picture in a dream.  Fear left her.  The human forms all round her lost their power.  They grew suffused and dim. . . . The pensive swing of the music changed to urgency and emphasis. . . . It came nearer and nearer.  It did not come from the candlelit corner where the piano was. . . . It came from everywhere.  It carried her out of the house, out of the world.

It hastened with her, on and on towards great brightness. . . . Everything was growing brighter and brighter. . . .

Gertrude Goldring, the Australian, was making noises with her hands like inflated paper bags being popped.  Miriam clutched her wool-needle and threaded it.  She drew the wool through her canvas, one, three, five, three, one and longed for the piano to begin again.

7

Clara Bergmann followed.  Miriam watched her as she took her place at the piano--how square and stout she looked and old, careworn, like a woman of forty.  She had high square shoulders and high square hips---her brow was low and her face thin and broad and flat.  Her eyes were like the eyes of a dog and her thin-lipped mouth long and straight until it went steadily down at the corners.  She wore a large fringe like Harriett's--and a thin coil of hair filled the nape of her neck.  She played, without music, her face lifted boldly.  The notes rang out in a prelude of unfinished phrases--the kind, Miriam noted, that had so annoyed her father in what he called new-fangled music--she felt it was going to be a brilliant piece--fireworks-

-execution--style--and sat up self-consciously and fixed her eyes on Clara's hands. "Can you see the hands?" she remembered having heard someone say at a concert. How easily they moved. Clara still sat back, her face raised to the light. The notes rang out like trumpet-calls as her hands dropped with an easy fling and sprang back and dropped again. What loose wrists she must have, thought Miriam. The clarion notes ceased. There was a pause. Clara threw back her head, a faint smile flickered over her face, her hands fell gently and the music came again, pianissimo, swinging in an even rhythm. It flowed from those clever hands, a half-indicated theme with a gentle, steady, throbbing undertow. Miriam dropped her eyes--she seemed to have been listening long--that wonderful light was coming again--she had forgotten her sewing--when presently she saw, slowly circling, fading and clearing, first its edge, and then, for a moment the whole thing, dripping, dripping as it circled, a weed-grown mill-wheel. . . . She recognised it instantly. She had seen it somewhere as a child--in Devonshire--and never thought of it since--and there it was. She heard the soft swish and drip of the water and the low humming of the wheel. How beautiful . . . it was fading. . . . She held it--it returned--clearer this time and she could feel the cool breeze it made, and sniff the fresh earthy scent of it, the scent of the moss and the weeds shining and dripping on its huge rim. Her heart filled. She felt a little tremor in her throat. All at once she knew that if she went on listening to that humming wheel and feeling the freshness of the air, she would cry. She pulled herself together, and for a while saw only a vague radiance in the room and the dim forms grouped about. She could not remember which was which. All seemed good and dear to her. The trumpet notes had come back, and in a few moments the music ceased. . . . Someone was closing the great doors from inside the schoolroom. As the side behind which she was sitting swung slowly to, she caught a glimpse, through the crack, of four boys with close-cropped heads, sitting at the long table. The gas was out and the room was dim, but a reading-lamp in the centre of the table cast its light on their bowed heads.

8

The playing of the two Martins brought back the familiar feeling of English self-consciousness. Solomon, the elder one, sat at her Beethoven sonata, an adagio movement, with a patch of dull crimson on the pallor of the cheek she presented to the room, but she played with a heavy fervour, preserving throughout the character-istic marching staccato of the bass, and gave unstinted value to the shading of each phrase.  She made Miriam feel nervous at first and then--as she went triumphantly forward and let herself go so tremendously--traction-engine, thought Miriam--in the heavy fortissimos,--a little ashamed of such expression coming from English hands.  The feeling of shame lingered as the younger sister followed with a spirited vivace.  Her hollow-cheeked pallor remained unstained, but her thin lips were set and her hard eyes were harder.  She played with determined nonchalance and an extraordinarily facile rapidity, and Miriam's uneasiness changed insensibly to the conviction that these girls were learning in Germany not to be ashamed of "playing with expression."  All the things she had heard Mr. Strood--who had, as the school prospectus declared, been "educated in Leipzig"--preach and implore, "style," "ex-pression," "phrasing," "light and shade," these girls were learning, picking up from these wonderful Germans.  They did not do it quite like them though.  They did not think only about the music, they thought about themselves too.  Miriam believed she could do it as the Germans did.  She wanted to get her own music and play it as she had always dimly known it ought to be played and hardly ever dared.  Perhaps that was how it was with the English.  They knew, but they did not dare.  No.  The two she had just heard playing were, she felt sure, imitating something--but hers would be no imitation.  She would play as she wanted to one day in this German atmosphere.  She wished now she were going to have lessons.  She had in fact had a lesson.  But she wanted to be alone and to play--or perhaps with someone in the next room listening.  Perhaps she would not have even the chance of practising.

9

Minna rippled through a Chopin valse that made Miriam think of an apple orchard in bloom against a blue sky, and was followed by Jimmie who played the Spring Song with slightly swaying body and little hands that rose and fell one against the other, and reminded Miriam of the finger game of her childhood--"Fly away Jack, fly away Jill."  She played very sweetly and surely except that now and again it was as if the music caught its breath.

Jimmie's Lied brought the piano solos to an end, and Fraulein Pfaff after a little speech of criticism and general encouragement asked, to Miriam's intense delight, for the singing. "Millie" was called for. Millie came out of a corner. She was out of Miriam's range at meal-times and appeared to her now for the first time as a tall child-girl in a high-waisted, blue serge frock, plainly made with long plain sleeves, at the end of which appeared two large hands shining red and shapeless with chilblains. She attracted Miriam at once with the shell-white and shell-pink of her complexion, her firm chubby baby-mouth and her wide gaze. Her face shone in the room, even her hair--done just like the Martins', but fluffy where theirs was flat and shiny--seemed to give out light, shadowy-dark though it was. Her figure was straight and flat, and she moved, thought Miriam, as though she had no feet.

She sang, with careful precision as to the accents of her German, in a high breathy effortless soprano, a little song about a child and a bouquet of garden flowers.

The younger Martin in a strong hard jolting voice sang of a love-sick Linden tree, her pale thin cheeks pink-flushed.

"Herr Kapellmeister chooses well," smiled Fraulein at the end of this performance.

The Vorspielen was brought to an end by Gertrude Goldring's song. Clara Bergmann sat down to accompany her, and Miriam roused herself for a double listening. There would be Clara's' opening and Clara's accompaniment and some wonderful song. The Australian stood well away from the piano, her shoulders thrown back and her eyes upon the wall opposite her. There was no prelude. Piano and voice rang out together--single notes which the voice took and sustained with an expressive power which was beyond anything in Miriam's experience. Not a note was quite true. . . . The unerring falseness of pitch was as startling as the quality of the voice. The great wavering shouts slurring now above, now below the mark amazed Miriam out of all shyness. She sat up, frankly gazing--"How dare she? She hasn't an atom of ear--how ghastly"--her thoughts exclaimed as the shouts went on. The longer sustained notes presently reminded her of something. It was like something she had heard--in the interval between the verses--while the sounds echoed in the mind she remembered the cry, hand to mouth, of a London dustman.

Then she lost everything in the story of the Sultan's daughter and the young

Asra, and when the fullest applause of the evening was going to Gertrude's song, she did not withhold her share.

10

Anna, the only servant Miriam had seen so far--an enormous woman whose face, apart from the small eyes, seemed all "bony structure," Miriam noted in a phrase borrowed from some unremembered reading--brought in a tray filled with cups of milk, a basket of white rolls and a pile of little plates. Gertrude took the tray and handed it about the room. As Miriam took her cup, chose a roll, deposited it on a plate and succeeded in abstracting the plate from the pile neatly, without fumbling, she felt that for the moment Gertrude was prepared to tolerate her. She did not desire this in the least, but when the deep harsh voice fell against her from the bending Australian, she responded to the "Wie gefallt's Ihnen?" with an upturned smile and a warm "sehr gut!" It gratified her to discover that she could, at the end of this one day, understand or at the worst gather the drift of, all she heard, both of German and French. Mademoiselle had exclaimed at her French--les mots si bien choisis--un accent sans faute--it must be ear. She must have a very good ear. And her English was all right--at least, if she chose. . . . Pater had always been worrying about slang and careless pronunciation. None of them ever said "cut in half" or "very unique" or "ho'sale" or "phodygraff." She was awfully slangy herself--she and Harriett were, in their thoughts as well as their words--but she had no provincialisms, no Londonisms--she could be the purest Oxford English. There was something at any rate to give her German girls. . . . She could say, "There are no rules for English pronunciation, but what is usual at the University of Oxford is decisive for cultured people"--"decisive for cultured people." She must remember that for the class.

"Na, was sticken Sie da Miss Henderson?"

It was Fraulein Pfaff.

Miriam who had as yet hardly spoken to her, did not know whether to stand or to remain seated. She half rose and then Fraulein Pfaff took the chair near her and Miriam sat down, stiff with fear. She could not remember the name of the thing she was making. She flushed and fumbled--thought of dressing-tables and the little objects of which she had made so many hanging to the mirror by ribbons; "toilet-tidies" haunted her--but that was not it--she smoothed out her work as if to show it to Fraulein--"Na, na," came the delicate caustic voice. "Was wird das wohl sein?" Then she remembered. "It's for a pin-cushion," she said. Surely she need, not venture on German with Fraulein yet.

"Ein Nadelkissen," corrected Fraulein, "das wird niedlich aussehen," she re-marked quietly, and then in English, "You like music, Miss Henderson?"

"Oh, yes," said Miriam, with a pounce in her voice.

"You play the piano?"

"A little."

"You must keep up your practice then, while you are with us--you must have time for practice."


## 11


Fraulein Pfaff rose and moved away. The girls were arranging the chairs in two rows--plates and cups were collected and carried away. It dawned on Miriam that they were going to have prayers. What a wet-blanket on her evening. Everything had been so bright and exciting so far. Obviously they had prayers every night. She felt exceedingly uncomfortable. She had never seen prayers in a sitting-room. It had been nothing at school--all the girls standing in the drill-room, rows of voices saying "adsum," then a Collect and the Lord's Prayer.

A huge Bible appeared on a table in front of Fraulein's high-backed chair. Mir-iam found herself ranged with the girls, sitting in an attentive hush. There was a quiet, slow turning of pages, and then a long indrawn sigh and Fraulein's clear, low, even voice, very gentle, not caustic now but with something child-like about it, "Und da kamen die Apostel zu Ihm. . . ." Miriam had a moment of revolt. She would not sit there and let a woman read the Bible at her . . . and in that "smarmy" way. . . . in spirit she rose and marched out of the room. As the English pupil-teacher bound to suffer all things or go home, she sat on. Presently her ear was charmed by Fraulein's slow clear enunciation, her pure unaspirated North German. It seemed to suit the narrative--and the narrative was new, vivid and real in this new tongue. She saw presently the little group of figures talking by the lake and was sorry when Fraulein's voice ceased.

Solomon Martin was at the piano. Someone handed Miriam a shabby little pa-
per-backed hymnbook. She fluttered the leaves. All the hymns appeared to have a
little short-lined verse, under each ordinary verse, in small print. It was in English-
-she read. She fumbled for the title-page and then her cheeks flamed with shame,
"Moody and Sankey." She was incredulous, but there it was, clearly enough. What
was such a thing doing here? . . . Finishing school for the daughters of gentlemen. .
. . She had never had such a thing in her hands before. . . . Fraulein could not know.
. . . She glanced at her, but Fraulein's cavernous mouth was serenely open and
the voices of the girls sang heartily, 'Whenhy-- *com*eth. Whenhy-- com</it>eth,
to *make*-up his *jew*els----" These girls, Germany, that piano. . . . What did the
English girls think? Had anyone said anything? Were they chapel? Fearfully, she
told them over. No. Judy might be, and the Martins perhaps, but not Gertrude, nor
Jimmie, nor Millie. How did it happen? What was the German Church? Luther-
-Lutheran.

She longed for the end.

She glanced through the book--frightful, frightful words and choruses.

The girls were getting on to their knees.

Oh dear, every night. Her elbows sank into soft red plush.

She was to have time for practising--and that English lesson--the first--Oxford,
decisive for--educated people. . . .

Fraulein's calm voice came almost in a whisper, "Vater unser . . . der Du bist im
Himmel," and the murmuring voices of the girls followed her.


## 12


Miriam went to bed content, wrapped in music. The theme of Carlo's solo recurred again and again; and every time it brought something of the wonderful light-
-the sense of going forward and forward through space. She fell asleep somewhere
outside the world. No sooner was she asleep than a voice was saying, "Bonjour,
Meece," and her eyes opened on daylight and Mademoiselle's little night-gowned
form minuetting towards her down the single strip of matting. Her hair, hanging in
short ringlets when released, fell forward round her neck as she bowed--the slight-

est dainty inclination, from side to side against the swaying of her dance.  She was smiling her down-glancing, little sprite smile.  Miriam loved her. . . .

A great plaque of sunlight lay across the breakfast-table.  Miriam was too happy to trouble about her imminent trial.  She reflected that it was quite possible to-day and to-morrow would be free.  None of the visiting masters came, except, sometimes, Herr Bossenberger for music-lessons--that much she had learned from Mademoiselle.  And, after all, the class she had so dreaded had dwindled to just these four girls, little Emma and the three grown-up girls.  They probably knew all the rules and beginnings.  It would be just reading and so on.  It would not be so terrible--four sensible girls; and besides they had accepted her.  It did not seem anything extraordinary to them that she should teach them; and they did not dislike her.  Of that she felt sure.  She could not say this for even one of the English girls.  But the German girls did not dislike her.  She felt at ease sitting amongst them and was glad she was there and not at the English end of the table.  Down here, hemmed in by the Bergmanns with Emma's little form, her sounds, movements and warmth, her little quiet friendliness planted between herself and the English, with the apparently unobservant Minna and Elsa across the way she felt safe.  She felt fairly sure those German eyes did not criticise her.  Perhaps, she suggested to herself, they thought a good deal of English people in general; and then they were in the minority, only four of them; it was evidently a school for English girls as much as anything . . . strange--what an adventure for all those English girls--to be just boarders--Miriam wondered how she would feel sitting there as an English boarder among the Martins and Gertrude, Millie, Jimmie and Judy?  It would mean being friendly with them.  Finally she ensconced herself amongst her Germans, feeling additionally secure. . . . Fraulein had spent many years in England.  Perhaps that explained the breakfast of oatmeal porridge--piled plates of thick stirabout thickly sprinkled with pale, very sweet powdery brown sugar--and the eggs to follow with rolls and butter.

Miriam wondered how Fraulein felt towards the English girls.

She wondered whether Fraulein liked the English girls best. . . . She paid no attention to the little spurts of conversation that came at intervals as the table grew more and more dismantled.  She was there, safely there--what a perfectly stupendous thing--"weird and stupendous" she told herself.  The sunlight poured over her and her companions from the great windows behind Fraulein Pfaff. . . .

## 14

When breakfast was over and the girls were clearing the table, Fraulein went to one of the great windows and stood for a moment with her hands on the hasp of the innermost of the double frames. "Balde, balde," Miriam heard her murmur, "werden wir offnen konnen." Soon, soon we may open. Obviously then they had had the windows shut all the winter. Miriam, standing in the corner near the companion window, wondering what she was supposed to do and watching the girls with an air--as nearly as she could manage--of indulgent condescension--saw, without turning, the figure at the window, gracefully tall, with a curious dignified pannier-like effect about the skirt that swept from the small tightly-fitting pointed bodice, reminding her of illustrations of heroines of serials in old numbers of the "Girls' Own Paper." The dress was of dark blue velvet--very much rubbed and faded. Miriam liked the effect, liked something about the clear profile, the sallow, hollow cheeks, the same heavy bonyness that Anna the servant had, but finer and redeemed by the wide eye that was so strange. She glanced fearfully, at its unconsciousness, and tried to find words for the quick youthfulness of those steady eyes.

Fraulein moved away into the little room opening from the schoolroom, and some of the girls joined her there. Miriam turned to the window. She looked down into a little square of high-walled garden. It was gravelled nearly all over. Not a blade of grass was to be seen. A narrow little border of bare brown mould joined the gravel to the high walls. In the centre was a little domed patch of earth and there a chestnut tree stood. Great bulging brown-varnished buds were shining whitely from each twig. The girls seemed to be gathering in the room behind her--settling down round the table--Mademoiselle's voice sounded from the head of the table where Fraulein had lately been. It must be *raccommodage* thought Miriam--the weekly mending Mademoiselle had told her of. Mademoiselle was superintending. Miriam listened. This was a sort of French lesson. They all sat round and did their mending together in French--darning must be quite different done like that, she reflected.

Jimmie's voice came, rounded and giggling, "Oh, Mademoiselle! j'ai une *po-*

*tato*, pardong, pum de terre, je mean." She poked three fingers through the toe of her stocking. "Veux dire, veux dire--Qu'est-ce-que vous me racontez la?" scolded Mademoiselle. Miriam envied her air of authority.

"Ah-ho! La-la--Boum--Bong!" came Gertrude's great voice from the door.

"Taisez-vous, taisez-vous, Jair-trude," rebuked Mademoiselle.

"How dare she?" thought Miriam, with a picture before her eyes of the little grey-gowned thing with the wistful, frugal mouth and nose.

"Na--Miss Henderson?"

It was Fraulein's voice from within the little room. Minna was holding the door open.

## 15

At the end of twenty minutes, dismissed by Fraulein with a smiling recommendation to go and practise in the saal, Miriam had run upstairs for her music.

"It's all right. I'm all right. I shall be able to do it," she said to herself as she ran. The ordeal was past. She was, she had learned, to talk English with the German girls, at table, during walks, whenever she found herself with them, excepting on Saturdays and Sundays--and she was to read with the four--for an hour, three times a week. There had been no mention of grammar or study in any sense she understood.

She had had a moment of tremor when Fraulein had said in her slow clear English, "I leave you to your pupils, Miss Henderson," and with that had gone out and shut the door. The moment she had dreaded had come. This was Germany. There was no escape. Her desperate eyes caught sight of a solid-looking volume on the table, bound in brilliant blue cloth. She got it into her shaking hands. It was "Misunderstood." She felt she could have shouted in her relief. A treatise on the Morse code would not have surprised her. She had heard that such things were studied at school abroad and that German children knew the names and, worse than that, the meaning of the names of the streets in the city of London. But this book that she and Harriett had banished and wanted to burn in their early teens together with "Sandford and Merton." . . .

"You are reading 'Misunderstood'?" she faltered, glancing at the four politely waiting girls.

It was Minna who answered her in her husky, eager voice.

"D'ja, d'ja," she responded, "na, ich meine, *yace, yace* we read--so sweet and beautiful book--not?"

"Oh," said Miriam, "yes . . ." and then eagerly, "you all like it, do you?"

Clara and Elsa agreed unenthusiastically. Emma, at her elbow, made a little despairing gesture, "I can't English," she moaned gently, "too deeficult."

Miriam tested their reading. The class had begun. Nothing had happened. It was all right. They each, dutifully and with extreme carefulness read a short passage. Miriam sat blissfully back. It was incredible. The class was going on. The chestnut tree budded approval from the garden. She gravely corrected their accents. The girls were respectful. They appeared to be interested. They vied with each other to get exact sounds; and they presently delighted Miriam by telling her they could understand her English much better than that of her predecessor. "So cleare, so cleare," they chimed, "Voonderfoll." And then they all five seemed to be talking at once. The little room was full of broken English, of Miriam's interpolated corrections. It was going--succeeding. This was her class. She hoped Fraulein was listening outside. She probably was. Heads of foreign schools did. She remembered Madame Beck in "Villette." But if she was not, she hoped they would tell her about being able to understand the new English teacher so well. "Oh, I am haypie," Emma was saying, with adoring eyes on Miriam and her two arms outflung on the table. Miriam recoiled. This would not do--they must not all talk at once and go on like this. Minna's whole face was aflame. She sat up stiffly--adjusted her pince-nez--and desperately ordered the reading to begin again--at Minna. They all subsided and Minna's careful husky voice came from her still blissfully-smiling face. The others sat back and attended. Miriam watched Minna judicially, and hoped she looked like a teacher. She knew her pince-nez disguised her and none of these girls knew she was only seventeen and a half. "Sorrowg," Minna was saying, hesitating. Miriam had not heard the preceding word. "Once more the whole sentence," she said, with quiet gravity, and then as Minna reached the word "thorough" she corrected and spent five minutes showing her how to get over the redoubtable "th." They all experimented and exclaimed. They had never been shown that it was just a matter of getting the tongue between the teeth. Miriam herself had only just discovered it. She speculated as to how long it would take her to deliver them up to Fraulein Pfaff with this notorious stumbling-block removed. She was astonished herself at the mechanical simplicity of the cure. How stupid people must be not to discover these things. Minna's voice went on. She would let her read a page. She began to wonder rather blankly what she was to do to fill up the hour after they had all read a page. She had just reached the conclusion that they must do some sort of writing when Fraulein Pfaff came, and still affable and smiling had ushered the girls to their mending and sent Miriam off to the saal.

## 16

As she flew upstairs for her music, saying, "I'm all right. I can do it all right," she was half-conscious that her provisional success with her class had very little to do with her bounding joy. That success had not so much given her anything to be glad about--it had rather removed an obstacle of gladness which was waiting to break forth. She was going to stay on. That was the point. She would stay in this wonderful place. . . . She came singing down through the quiet house--the sunlight poured from bedroom windows through open doors. She reached the quiet saal. Here stood the great piano, its keyboard open under the light of the French window opposite the door through which she came. Behind the great closed swing doors the girls were talking over their raccommodage. Miriam paid no attention to them. She would ignore them all. She did not even need to try to ignore them. She felt strong and independent. She would play, to herself. She would play something she knew perfectly, a Grieg lyric or a movement from a Beethoven Sonata . . . on this gorgeous piano . . . and let herself go, and listen. That was music . . . not playing things, but listening to Beethoven. . . . It must be Beethoven . . . Grieg was different . . . acquired . . . like those strange green figs Pater had brought from Tarring . . . Beethoven had always been real.

It was all growing clearer and clearer. . . . She chose the first part of the first movement of the Sonata Pathetique. That she knew she could play faultlessly. It was the last thing she had learned, and she had never grown weary of practising slowly through its long bars of chords. She had played it at her last music-lesson . . . dear old Stroodie walking up and down the long drilling-room. . . . "Steady the bass"; "grip the chords," then standing at her side and saying in the thin light sneery part of his voice, "You can . . . you've got hands like umbrellas" . . . and showing her how easily she could stretch two notes beyond his own span.  And then marching away as she played and crying out to her standing under the high windows at the far end of the room, "Let it go!  Let it go!"

And she had almost forgotten her wretched self, almost heard the music. . . .

She felt for the pedals, lifted her hands a span above the piano as Clara had done and came down, true and clean, on to the opening chord.  The full rich tones of the piano echoed from all over the room; and some metal object far away from her hummed the dominant.  She held the chord for its full term. . . . Should she play any more?

She had confessed herself . . . just that minor chord . . . anyone hearing it would know more than she could ever tell them . . . her whole being beat out the rhythm as she waited for the end of the phrase to insist on what already had been said.  As it came, she found herself sitting back, slackening the muscles of her arms and of her whole body, and ready to swing forward into the rising storm of her page.  She did not need to follow the notes on the music stand.  Her fingers knew them.  Grave and happy she sat with unseeing eyes, listening, for the first time.

At the end of the page she was sitting with her eyes full of tears, aware of Fraulein standing between the open swing doors with Gertrude's face showing over her shoulder--its amazement changing to a large-toothed smile as Fraulein's quietly repeated "Prachtvoll, prachtvoll" came across the room.  Miriam, after a hasty smile, sat straining her eyes as widely as possible, so that the tears should not fall.  She glared at the volume in front of her, turning the pages.  She was glad that the heavy sun-blinds cast a deep shadow over the room.  She blinked.  She thought they would not notice.  Only one tear fell and that was from the left eye, towards the wall.  "You are a real musician, Miss Henderson," said Fraulein, advancing.

17

Every other day or so Miriam found she could get an hour on a bedroom piano; and always on a Saturday morning during *raccommodage.*  She rediscovered all the pieces she had already learned.

She went through them one by one, eagerly, slurring over difficulties, pressing on, getting their effect, listening and discovering. "It's *technique* I want," she told herself, when she had reached the end of her collection, beginning to attach a meaning to the familiar word. Then she set to work. She restricted herself to the Pathetique, always omitting the first page, which she knew so well and practised mechanically, slowly, meaninglessly, with neither pedalling nor expression, page by page until a movement was perfect. Then when the mood came, she played . . . and listened. She soon discovered she could not always "play"--even the things she knew perfectly--and she began to understand the fury that had seized her when her mother and a woman here and there had taken for granted one should "play when asked," and coldly treated her refusal as showing lack of courtesy. "Ah!" she said aloud, as this realisation came, "Women."

"Of course you can only 'play when you *can,*'" said she to herself, "like a bird singing."

She sang once or twice, very quietly, in those early weeks. But she gave that up. She had a whole sheaf of songs with her. But after that first Vorspielen they seemed to have lost their meaning. One by one she looked them through. Her dear old Venetian song, "Beauty's Eyes," "An Old Garden"--she hesitated over that, and hummed it through--"Best of All"--"In Old Madrid"--the vocal score of the "Mikado"--her little "Chanson de Florian," and a score of others. She blushed at her collection. The "Chanson de Florian" might perhaps hold its own at a Vorspielen-- sung by Bertha Martin--perhaps. . . . The remainder of her songs, excepting a little bound volume of Sterndale Bennett, she put away at the bottom of her Saratoga trunk. Meanwhile, there were songs being learned by Herr Bossenberger's pupils for which she listened hungrily; Schubert, Grieg, Brahms. She would always, during those early weeks, sacrifice her practising to listen from the schoolroom to a pupil singing in the saal.

18

The morning of Ulrica Hesse's arrival was one of the mornings when she could "play." She was sitting, happy, in the large English bedroom, listening. It was late. She was beginning to wonder why the gonging did not come when the door opened. It was Millie in her dressing-gown, with her hair loose and a towel over her arm.

"Oh, bitte, Miss Henderson, will you please go down to Frau Krause, Fraulein Pfaff says," she said, her baby face full of responsibility.

Miriam rose uneasily. What might this be? "Frau Krause?" she asked.

"Oh yes, it's Haarwaschen," said Millie anxiously, evidently determined to wait until Miriam recognised her duty.

"Where?" said Miriam aghast.

"Oh, in the basement. I *must* go. Frau Krause's waiting. Will you come?"

"Oh well, I suppose so," mumbled Miriam, coming to the door as the child turned to go.

"All right," said Millie, "I'm going down. Do make haste, Miss Henderson, will you?"

"All right," said Miriam, going back into the room.

Collecting her music she went incredulously upstairs. This was school with a vengeance. This was boarding-school. It was abominable. Fraulein Pfaff indeed! Ordering her, Miriam, to go downstairs and have her hair washed . . . by Frau Krause . . . off-hand, without any warning . . . someone should have told her--and let her choose. Her hair was clean. Sarah had always done it. Miriam's throat contracted. She would not go down. Frau Krause should not touch her. She reached the attics. Their door was open and there was Mademoiselle in her little alpaca dressing-jacket, towelling her head.

Her face came up, flushed and gay. Miriam was too angry to note till afterwards how pretty she had looked with her hair like that.

"Ah! . . . c'est le grand lavage!" sang Mademoiselle.

"Oui," said Miriam surlily.

What could she do? She imagined the whole school waiting downstairs to see her come down to be done. Should she go down and decline, explain to Fraulein Pfaff. She hated her vindictively--her "calm" message--"treating me like a child." She saw the horse smile and heard the caustic voice.

"It's sickening," she muttered, whisking her dressing-gown from its nail and seizing a towel. Mademoiselle was piling up her damp hair before the little mirror.

Slowly Miriam made her journey to the basement.

Minna and Elsa were brushing out their long hair with their door open. A strong sweet perfume came from the room.

The basement hall was dark save for the patch of light coming from the open kitchen door. In the patch stood a low table and a kitchen chair. On the table which was shining wet and smeary with soap, stood a huge basin. Out over the basin flew a long tail of hair and Miriam's anxious eyes found Millie standing in the further gloom twisting and wringing.

## 19

No one else was to be seen. Perhaps it was all over. She was too late. Then a second basin held in coarse red hands appeared round the kitchen door and in a moment a woman, large and coarse, with the sleeves of her large-checked blue and white cotton dress rolled back and a great "teapot" of pale nasturtium coloured hair shining above the third of Miriam's "bony" German faces had emerged and plumped her steaming basin down upon the table.

Soap? and horrid pudding basins of steaming water. Miriam's hair had never been washed with anything but cantharides and rose-water on a tiny special sponge.

In full horror, "Oh," she said, in a low vague voice, "It doesn't matter about me."

"Gun' Tak' Fr'n," snapped the woman briskly.

Miriam gave herself up.

"Gooten Mawgen, Frau Krause," said Millie's polite departing voice.

Miriam's outraged head hung over the steaming basin--her hair spread round it like a tent frilling out over the table.

For a moment she thought that the nausea which had seized her as she surrendered would, the next instant, make flight imperative. Then her amazed ears caught the sharp bump--crack--of an eggshell against the rim of the basin, followed by a further brisk crackling just above her. She shuddered from head to foot as the egg descended with a cold slither upon her incredulous skull. Tears came to her eyes as she gave beneath the onslaught of two hugely enveloping, vigorously drubbing hands--"sh--ham--poo" gasped her mind.

The drubbing went relentlessly on. Miriam steadied her head against it and gradually warmth and ease began to return to her shivering, clenched body. Her hair was gathered into the steaming basin--dipped and rinsed and spread, a comforting compress, warm with the water, over her egg-sodden head. There was more drubbing, more dipping and rinsing. The second basin was re-filled from the kitchen, and after a final rinse in its fresh warm water, Miriam found herself standing up--with a twisted tail of wet hair hanging down over her cape of damp towel--glowing and hungry.

"Thank you," she said timidly to Frau Krause's bustling presence.

"Gun' Tak Fr'n," said Frau Krause, disappearing into the kitchen.

Miriam gave her hair a preliminary drying, gathered her dressing-gown together and went upstairs. From the schoolroom came unmistakable sounds. They were evidently at dinner. She hurried to her attic. What *was* she to do with her hair? She rubbed it desperately--fancy being landed with hair like that, in the middle of the day! She could not possibly go down. . . . She must. Fraulein Pfaff would expect her to--and would be disgusted if she were not quick--she towelled frantically at the short strands round her forehead, despairingly screwed them into Hinde's and towelled at the rest. What had the other girls done? If only she could look into the schoolroom before going down--it was awful--what should she do? . . . She caught sight of a sodden-looking brush on Mademoiselle's bed. Mademoiselle had put hers up--she had seen her . . . of course . . . easy enough for her little fluffy clouds--she could do nothing with her straight, wet lumps--she began to brush it out--it separated into thin tails which flipped tiny drops of moisture against her hands as she brushed. Her arms ached; her face flared with her exertions. She was ravenous--she must manage somehow and go down. She braided the long strands and fastened their cold mass with extra hairpins. Then she unfastened the Hinde's--two tendrils flopped limply against her forehead. She combed them out. They fell in a curtain of streaks to her nose. Feverishly she divided them, draped them somehow back into the rest of her hair and fastened them.

"Oh," she breathed, "my *ghastly* forehead."

It was all she could do--short of gas and curling tongs. Even the candle was taken away in the daytime.

It was cold and bleak upstairs. Her wet hair lay in a heavy mass against her burning head. She was painfully hungry. She went down.

20

The snarling rattle of the coffee mill sounded out into the hall. Several voices were speaking together as she entered. Fraulein Pfaff was not there. Gertrude Goldring was grinding the coffee. The girls were sitting round the table in easy attitudes and had the effect of holding a council. Emma, her elbows on the table, her little face bunched with scorn, put out a motherly arm and set a chair for Miriam. Jimmie had flung some friendly remark as she came in. Miriam did not hear what she said, but smiled responsively. She wanted to get quietly to her place and look round. There was evidently something in the air. They all seemed preoccupied. Perhaps no one would notice how awful she looked. "You're not the only one, my dear," she said to herself in her mother's voice. "No," she replied in person, "but no one will be looking so perfectly frightful as me."

"I say, do they know you're down?" said Gertrude hospitably, as the boiling water snored on to the coffee.

Emma rushed to the lift and rattled the panel.

"Anna!" she ordered, "Meece Hendshon! Suppe!"

"Oh, thanks," said Miriam, in general. She could not meet anyone's eye. The coffee cups were being slid up to Gertrude's end of the table and rapidly filled by her. Gertrude, of course, she noticed had contrived to look dashing and smart. Her hair, with the exception of some wild ends that hung round her face was screwed loosely on the top of her head and transfixed with a dagger-like tortoise-shell hair ornament--like a Japanese--Indian--no, Maori--that was it, she looked like a New Zealander. Clara and Minna had fastened up theirs with combs and ribbons and looked decent--frauish though, thought Miriam. Judy wore a plait. Without her fuzzy cloud she looked exactly like a country servant, a farmhouse servant. She drank her coffee noisily and furtively--she looked extraordinary, thought Miriam, and took comfort. The Martins' brown bows appeared on their necks instead of cresting their heads-it improved them, Miriam thought. What regular features they had. Bertha looked like a youth--like a musician. Her hair was loosened a little at the sides, shading the corners of her forehead and adding to its height. It shone like marble, high and straight. Emma's hair hung round her like a shawl. 'Lisbeth, Gretchen . . . what was that lovely German name . . . hild . . . Brunhilde. . .

Talk had begun again. Miriam hoped they had not noticed her. Her "Braten" shot up the lift.

"Lauter Unsinn!" announced Clara.

"We've all got to do our hair in clash . . . clashishsher Knoten, Hendy, all of us," said Jimmie judicially, sitting forward with her plump hands clasped on the table. Her pinnacle of hair looked exactly as usual.

"Oh, really." Miriam tried to make a picture of a classic knot in her mind.

"If one have classic head one can have classic knot," scolded Clara.

"Who have classic head?"

"How many classic head in the school of Waldstrasse?"

Elsa gave a little neighing laugh. "Classisch head, classisch Knote."

"That is true what you say, Clarah."

The table paused.

"Dites-moi--qu'est-ce-que ce terrible classique notte? Dites!"

No one seemed prepared to answer Mademoiselle's challenge.

Miriam's mind groped . . . classic--Greece and Rome--Greek knot. . . . Grecian key . . . a Grecian key pattern on the dresses for the sixth form tableau--reading Ruskin . . . the strip of glass all along the window space on the floor in the large room--edged with mosses and grass--the mirror of Venus. . . .

"Eh bien? Eh bien!"

. . . Only the eldest pretty girls . . . all on their hands and knees looking into the mirror. . . .

"Classische Form--Griechisch," explained Clara.

"Like a statue, Mademoiselle."

"Comment! Une statue! Je dois arranger mes cheveux comme une statue? Oh, ciel!" mocked Mademoiselle, collapsing into tinkles of her sprite laughter. . . . "Oh-la-la! Et quelle statue par exemple?" she trilled, with ironic eyebrows, "la statue de votre Kaisere Wilhelm der Grosse peut-etre?"

The Martins' guffaws led the laughter.

"Mademoisellekin with her hair done like the Kaiser Wilhelm," pealed Jimmie.

Only Clara remained grave in wrath.

"Einfach," she quoted bitterly, "Simple--says Lily, so simple!"
Simple--simpler--simplicissimusko!"

"I make no change, not at all," smiled Minna from behind her nose. "For this Ulrica it is quite something other. . . . She has yes truly so charming a little head."

She spoke quietly and unenviously.

"I too, indeed. Lily may go and play the flute."

"Brave girls," said Gertrude, getting up. "Come on, Kinder, clearing time. You'll excuse us, Miss Henderson? There's your pudding in the lift. Do you mind having your coffee *mit?*"

The girls began to clear up.

*"Leelly, Leely,* Leely Pfaff," muttered Clara as she helped, "so einfach und niedlich," she mimicked, "ach *was!* Schwarmerei--das find' ich abscheulich! I find it disgusting!"

So that was it. It was the new girl. Lily, was Fraulein Pfaff. So the new girl wore her hair in a classic knot. How lovely. Without her hat she had "a charming little head," Minna had said. And that face. Minna had seen how lovely she was and had not minded. Clara was jealous. Her head with a classic knot and no fringe, her worn-looking sallow face. . . . She would look like a "prisoner at the bar" in some newspaper. How they hated Fraulein Pfaff. The Germans at least. Fancy calling her Lily Miriam did not like it, she had known at once. None of the teachers at school had been called by their Christian names--there had been old Quagmire, the Elfkin, and dear Donnikin, Stroodie, and good old Kingie and all of them--but no Christian names. Oh yes--Sally--so there had--Sally--but then Sally was--couldn't have been anything else--never could have held a position of any sort. They ought not to call Fraulein Pfaff that. It was, somehow, nasty. Did the English girls do it? Ought she to have said anything? Mademoiselle did not seem at all shocked. Where was Fraulein Pfaff all this time? Perhaps somewhere hidden away, in her rooms, being "done" by Frau Krause. Fancy telling them all to alter the way they did their hair.

21

Everyone was writing Saturday letters--Mademoiselle and the Germans with compressed lips and fine careful evenly moving pen-points; the English scrawling and scraping and dashing, their pens at all angles and careless, eager faces.  An almost unbroken silence seemed the order of the earlier part of a Saturday afternoon. To-day the room was very still, save for the slight movements of the writers.  At intervals nothing was to be heard but the little chorus of pens.  Clara, still smouldering, sitting at the window end of the room looked now and again gloomily out into the garden.  Miriam did not want to write letters.  She sat, pen in hand, and note-paper in front of her, feeling that she loved the atmosphere of these Saturday afternoons.  This was her second.  She had been in the school a fortnight--the first Saturday she had spent writing to her mother--a long letter for everyone to read, full of first impressions and enclosing a slangy almost affectionate little note for Harriett.  In her general letter she had said, "If you want to think of something jolly, think of me, here."  She had hesitated over that sentence when she considered meal-times, especially the midday meal, but on the whole she had decided to let it stand--this afternoon she felt it was truer.  She was beginning to belong to the house--she did not want to write letters--but just to sit revelling in the sense of this room full of quietly occupied girls--in the first hours of the weekly holiday.  She thought of strange Ulrica somewhere upstairs and felt quite one of the old gang. "Ages" she had known all these girls.  She was not afraid of them at all.  She would not be afraid of them any more.  Emma Bergmann across the table raised a careworn face from her two lines of large neat lettering and caught her eye.  She put up her hands on either side of her mouth as if for shouting.

"*Hendchen,*" she articulated silently, in her curious lipless way, "mein liebes, liebes, Hendchen."

Miriam smiled timidly and sternly began fumbling at her week's letters--one from Eve, full of congratulations and recommendations--"Keep up your music, my dear," said the conclusion, "and don't mind that little German girl being fond of you.  It is impossible to be too fond of people if you keep it all on a high level," and a scrawl from Harriett, pure slang from beginning to end.  Both these letters and an earlier one from her mother had moved her to tears and longing when they came. She re-read them now unmoved and felt aloof from the things they suggested. It did not seem imperative to respond to them at once. She folded them together. If only she could bring them all for a minute into this room, the wonderful Germany that she had achieved. If they could even come to the door and look in. She did not in the least want to go back. She wanted them to come to her and taste Germany--to see all that went on in this wonderful house, to see pretty, German Emma, adoring her--to hear the music that was everywhere all the week, that went, like a garland, in and out of everything, to hear her play, by accident, and acknowledge the difference in her playing. Oh yes, besides seeing them all she wanted them to hear her play. . . . She must stay . . . she glanced round the room. It was here, somehow, somewhere, in this roomful of girls, centring in the Germans at her end of the table, reflected on to the English group, something of that influence that had made her play. It was in the sheen on Minna's hair, in Emma's long-plaited school-girlishness, somehow in Clara's anger. It was here, here, and she was in it. . . . She must pretend to be writing letters or someone might speak to her. She would hate anyone who challenged her at this moment. Jimmie might. It was just the kind of thing Jimmie would do. Her eyes were always roving round. . . . There were a lot of people like that. . . . It was all right when you wanted anything or to--to--"create a diversion"--when everybody was quarrelling. But at the wrong times it was awful. . . . The Radnors and Pooles were like that. She could have killed them often. "Hul-lo, Mim," they would say. "Wake up!" or "What's the row!" and if you asked why, they would laugh and tell you you looked like a dying duck in a thunderstorm. . . . It was all right. No one had noticed her--or if either of the Germans had they would not think like that--they would understand--she believed in a way, they would understand. At the worst they would look at you as if they were somehow with you and say something sentimental. "Sie hat Heimweh" or something like that. Minna would. Minna's forget-me-not blue eyes behind her pink nose would be quite real and alive. . . . Ein Blatt--she dipped her pen and wrote Ein Blatt . . . aus . . . Ein Blatt aus sommerlichen Tagen that thing they had begun last Saturday afternoon and gone on and on with until she had hated the sound of the words. How did it go on? "Ein Blatt aus sommerlichen Tagen," she breathed in a half whisper. Minna heard--and without looking up from her writing quietly repeated the verse. Her voice rose and trembled slightly on the last line.

"Oh, chuck it, Minna," groaned Bertha Martin.

"Tchookitt," repeated Minna absently, and went on with her writing.

Miriam was scribbling down the words as quickly as she could--

"Ein Blatt aus sommerlichen Tagen Ich nahm es so im Wandern mit Auf dass es einst mir moge sagen Wie laut die Nachtigall geschlagen Wie grun der Wald den ich--durchtritt--"

durchtritt--durchschritt--she was not sure.  It was perfectly lovely--she read it through translating stumblingly--

"A leaf from summery days I took it with me on my way, So that it might re-mind me How loud the nightingale had sung, How green the wood I had passed through."

With a pang she felt it was true that summer ended in dead leaves.

But she had no leaf, nothing to remind her of her summer days.  They were all past and she had nothing--not the smallest thing.  The two little bunches of flow-ers she had put away in her desk had all crumbled together, and she could not tell which was which. . . . There was nothing else but the things she had told Eve--and perhaps Eve had forgotten . . . there was nothing.  There were the names in her birthday book!  She had forgotten them.  She would look at them.  She flushed. She would look at them to-morrow, sometime when Mademoiselle was not there. . . . The room was waking up from its letter-writing.  People were moving about. She would not write to-day.  It was not worth while beginning.  She took a fresh sheet of note-paper and copied her verse, spacing it carefully with a wide margin all round so that it came exactly in the middle of the page.  It would soon be tea-time. "Wie grun der Wald."  She remembered one wood--the only one she could remem-ber--there were no woods at Barnes or at the seaside--only that wood, at the very beginning, someone carrying Harriett--and green green, the brightest she had ever seen, and anemones everywhere, she could see them distinctly at this moment--she wanted to put her face down into the green among the anemones.  She could not remember how she got there or the going home, but just standing there--the green and the flowers and something in her ear buzzing and frightening her and making her cry, and somebody poking a large finger into the buzzing ear and making it very hot and sore.

The afternoon sitting had broken up.  The table was empty.

Emma, in raptures--near the window, was calling to the other Germans.  Minna came and chirruped too--there was a sound of dull scratching on the window--then a little burst of admiration from Emma and Minna together.  Miriam looked round--in Emma's hand shone a small antique watch encrusted with jewels; at her side was the new girl.  Miriam saw a filmy black dress, and above it a pallid face.  What was it like?  It was like--like--like jasmine--that was it--jasmine--and out of the jasmine face the great gaze she had met in the morning turned half-puzzled, half-disappointed upon the growing group of girls examining the watch.

## CHAPTER IV

### 1

Miriam paid her first visit to a German church the next day, her third Sunday. Of the first Sunday, now so far off, she could remember nothing but sitting in a low-backed chair in the saal trying to read "Les Travailleurs de la Mer" . . . seas . . . and a sunburnt youth striding down a desolate lane in a storm . . . and the beginning of tea-time. They had been kept indoors all day by the rain.

The second Sunday they had all gone in the evening to the English church with Fraulein Pfaff . . . rush-seated chairs with a ledge for books, placed very close together and scrooping on the stone floor with the movements of the congregation . . . a little gathering of English people. They seemed very dear for a moment . . . what was it about them that was so attractive . . . that gave them their air of "refinement"? . . .

Then as she watched their faces as they sang she felt that she knew all these women, the way, with little personal differences, they would talk, the way they would smile and take things for granted.

And the men, standing there in their overcoats. . . . Why were they there? What were they doing? What were their thoughts?

She pressed as against a barrier. Nothing came to her from these unconscious forms.

They seemed so untroubled. . . . Probably they were all Conservatives. . . . That was part of their "refinement." They would all disapprove of Mr. Gladstone. . . . Get up into the pulpit and say "Gladstone" very loud . . . and watch the result. Gladstone was a Radical . . . "pull everything up by the roots." . . . Pater was always angry and sneery about him. . . . Where were the Radicals? Somewhere very far away . . . tub-thumping . . . the Conservatives made them thump tubs . . . no wonder.

She decided she must be a Radical. Certainly she did not belong to these "refined" English--women or men. She was quite sure of that, seeing them gathered together, English Church-people in this foreign town.

But then Radicals were probably chapel?

It would be best to stay with the Germans. Yes. . . . she would stay. There was a woman sitting in the endmost chair just across the aisle in line with them. She had a pale face and looked worn and middle-aged. The effect of "refinement" made on Miriam by the congregation seemed to radiate from her. There was a large ostrich feather fastened by a gleaming buckle against the side of her silky beaver hat. It swept, Miriam found the word during the Psalms, back over her hair. Miriam glancing at her again and again felt that she would like to be near her, watch her and touch her and find out the secret of her effect. But not talk to her, never talk to her.

She, too, sad and alone though Miriam knew her to be, would have her way of smiling and taking things for granted. The sermon came. Miriam sat, chafing, through it. One angry glance towards the pulpit had shown her a pale, black-moustached face. She checked her thoughts. She felt they would be too savage; would rend her unendurably. She tried not to listen. She felt the preacher was dealing out "pastoral platitudes." She tried to give her mind elsewhere; but the sound of the voice, unconvinced and unconvincing threatened her again and again with a tide of furious resentment. She fidgeted and felt for thoughts and tried to compose her face to a semblance of serenity. It would not do to sit scowling here amongst her pupils with Fraulein Pfaff's eye commanding her profile from the end of the pew just behind. . . . The air was gassy and close, her feet were cold. The gentle figure across the aisle was sitting very still, with folded hands and grave eyes fixed in the direction of the pulpit. Of course. Miriam had known it. She would "think over" the sermon afterwards. . . . The voice in the pulpit had dropped. Miriam glanced up. The figure faced about and intoned rapidly, the congregation rose for a moment rustling, and rustling subsided again. A hymn was given out. They rose again and sang. It was "Lead, Kindly Light." Chilly and feverish and weary Miriam listened . . . "the encircling glooo--om" . . . Cardinal Newman coming back from Italy in a

ship . . . in the end he had gone over to Rome . . . high altars . . . candles . . . incense
. . . safety and warmth.

From far away a radiance seemed to approach and to send out a breath that
touched and stirred the stuffy air . . . the imploring voices sang on . . . poor cold
English things . . . Miriam suddenly became aware of Emma Bergmann standing at
her side with open hymn-book shaking with laughter. She glanced sternly at her,
mastering a sympathetic convulsion.

2

Emma looked so sweet standing there shaking and suffused. Her blue eyes
were full of tears. Miriam wanted to giggle too. She longed to know what had
amused her . . . just the fact of their all standing suddenly there together. She dared
not join her . . . no more giggling as she and Harriett had giggled. She would not
even be able afterwards to ask her what it was.

3

Sitting on this third Sunday morning in the dim Schloss Kirche--the Waldstrasse pew was in one of its darkest spaces and immediately under the shadow of
a deeply overhanging gallery--Miriam understood poor Emma's confessed hyste-
ria over the abruptly alternating kneelings and standings, risings and sittings of an
Anglican congregation. Here, there was no need to be on the watch for the next
move. The service droned quietly and slowly on. Miriam paid no heed to it. She
sat in the comforting darkness. The unobserving Germans were all round her, the
English girls tailed away invisibly into the distant obscurity. Fraulein Pfaff was
not there, nor Mademoiselle. She was alone with the school. She felt safe for a
while and derived solace from the reflection that there would always be church.
If she were a governess all her life there would be church. There was a little sting
of guilt in the thought. It would be practising deception. . . . To despise it all, to
hate the minister and the choir and the congregation and yet to come--running--
she could imagine herself all her life running, at least in her mind, weekly to some
church--working her fingers into their gloves and pretending to take everything

for granted and to be just like everybody else and really thinking only of getting into a quiet pew and ceasing to pretend. It was wrong to use church like that. She was wrong--all wrong. It couldn't be helped. Who was there who could help her? She imagined herself going to a clergyman and saying she was bad and wanted to be good--even crying. He would be kind and would pray and smile--and she would be told to listen to sermons in the right spirit. She could never do that. . . . There she felt she was on solid ground. Listening to sermons was wrong . . . people ought to refuse to be preached at by these men. Trying to listen to them made her more furious than anything she could think of, more base in submitting . . . those men's sermons were worse than women's smiles . . . just as insincere at any rate . . . and you could get away from the smiles, make it plain you did not agree and that things were not simple and settled . . . but you could not stop a sermon. It was so unfair. The service might be lovely, if you did not listen to the words; and then the man got up and went on and on from unsound premises until your brain was sick . . . droning on and on and getting more and more pleased with himself and emphatic . . . and nothing behind it. As often as not you could pick out the logical fallacy if you took the trouble. . . . Preachers knew no more than anyone else . . . you could see by their faces . . . sheeps' faces. . . . What a terrible life . . . and wives and children in the homes taking them for granted. . . .

4

Certainly it was wrong to listen to sermons . . . stultifying . . . unless they were intellectual . . . lectures like Mr. Brough's . . . that was as bad, because they were not sermons. . . . either kind was bad and ought not to be allowed . . . a homily . . . sermons . . . homilies . . . a quiet homily might be something rather nice . . . and have not *Charity*--sounding brass and tinkling cymbal. . . . Caritas . . . I have **none** I am sure. . . . Fraulein Pfaff would listen. She would smile afterwards and talk about a "schone Predigt"--certainly. . . . If she should ask about the sermon? Everything would come out then.

What would be the good? Fraulein would not understand. It would be better to pretend. She could not think of any woman who would understand. And she would be obliged to live somewhere. She must pretend to somebody. She wanted to go on, to see the spring. But must she always be pretending? Would it always be that . . . living with exasperating women who did not understand . . . pretending . . . grimacing? . . . Were German women the same? She wished she could tell Eve the things she was beginning to feel about women. These English girls were just the same. Millie . . . sweet lovely Millie. . . . How she wished she had never spoken to her. Never said, "Are you fond of crochet?" . . . Millie saying, "You must know all my people," and then telling her a list of names and describing all her family. She had been so pleased for the first moment. It had made her feel suddenly happy to hear an English voice talking familiarly to her in the saal. And then at the end of a few moments she had known she never wanted to hear anything more of Millie and her people. It seemed strange that this girl talking about her brothers' hobbies and the colour of her sister's hair was the Millie she had first seen the night of the Vorspielen with the "Madonna" face and no feet. Millie was smug. Millie would smile when she was a little older--and she would go respectfully to church all her life--Miriam had felt a horror even of the work-basket Millie had been tidying dur-ing their conversation--and Millie had gone upstairs, she knew, feeling that they had "begun to be friends" and would be different the next time they met. It was her own fault. What had made her speak to her? She was like that. . . . Eve had told her. She got excited and interested in people and then wanted to throw them up. It was not true. She did not want to throw them up. She wanted them to leave her alone. . . . She had not been excited about Millie. It was Ulrica . . . Ulrica . . . Ulrica . . . Ulrica . . . sitting up at breakfast with her lovely head and her great eyes--her thin fingers peeling an egg. . . . She had made them all look so "common." Ulrica was different. Was she? Yes, Ulrica was different . . . Ulrica peeling an egg and she, afterwards like a mad thing had gone into the saal and talked to Millie in a vulgar, familiar way, no doubt.

And that had led to that dreadful talk with Gertrude. Gertrude's voice sound-ing suddenly behind her as she stood looking out of the saal window and their talk. She wished Gertrude had not told her about Hugo Wieland and the skating. She was sure she would not have liked Erica Wieland. She was glad she had left. "She was my chum," Gertrude had said, "and he taught us all the outside edge and taught me figure-skating."

It was funny--improper--that these schoolgirls should go skating with other girls' brothers. She had been so afraid of Gertrude that she had pretended to be interested and had joked with her--she, Miss Henderson, the governess had said-- knowingly, "Let's see, he's the clean-shaven one, isn't he?"

" *Rather*," Gertrude had said with a sort of winking grimace. . . .

5

They were singing a hymn. The people near her had not moved. Nobody had moved. The whole church was sitting down, singing a hymn. What wonderful people. . . . Like a sort of tea-party . . . everybody sitting about--not sitting up to the table . . . happy and comfortable.

Emma had found her place and handed her a big hymn-book with the score.

There was time for Miriam to read the first line and recognise the original of "Now thank we all our God',' before the singing had reached the third syllable. She hung over the book. "Nun--dank--et--Al--le--Gott." Now--thank--all--God. She read that first line again and felt how much better the thing was without the "we" and the "our." What a perfect phrase. . . . The hymn rolled on and she recognised that it was the tune she knew--the hard square tune she and Eve had called it--and Harriett used to mark time to it in jerks, a jerk to each syllable, with a twisted glove-finger tip just under the book ledge with her left hand, towards Miriam. But sung as these Germans sang it, it did not jerk at all. It did not sound like a "proclamation" or an order. It was . . . somehow . . . everyday. The notes seemed to hold her up. This was--Luther--Germany--the Reformation--solid and quiet. She glanced up and then hung more closely over her book. It was the stained-glass windows that made the Schloss Kirche so dark. One movement of her head showed her that all the windows within sight were dark with rich colour, and there was oak every-where--great shelves and galleries and juttings of dark wood, great carved masses and a high dim roof, and strange spaces of light; twilight, and light like moonlight and people, not many people, a troop, a little army under the high roof, with the great shadows all about them. "Nun danket alle Gott." There was nothing to object to in that. Everybody could say that. Everybody--Fraulein, Gertrude, all these little figures in the church, the whole world. "Now thank, all, God!" . . . Emma and Marie were chanting on either side of her. Immediately behind her sounded the

quavering voice of an old woman.  They all felt it.  She must remember that. . . .
Think of it every day.

## CHAPTER V

### 1

During those early days Miriam realised that school-routine, as she knew it--the planned days--the regular unvarying succession of lessons and preparations, had no place in this new world. Even the masters' lessons, coming in from outside and making a kind of framework of appointments over the otherwise fortuitously occupied days, were, she soon found, not always securely calculable. Herr Kapellmeister Bossenberger would be heard booming and intoning in the hall unexpectedly at all hours. He could be heard all over the house. Miriam had never seen him, but she noticed that great haste was always made to get a pupil to the saal and that he taught impatiently. He shouted and corrected and mimicked. Only Millie's singing, apparently, he left untouched. You could hear her lilting away through her little high songs as serenely as she did at Vorspielen.

Miriam was at once sure that he found his task of teaching these girls an extremely tiresome one.

Probably most teachers found teaching tiresome. But there was something peculiar and new to her in Herr Bossenberger's attitude. She tried to account for it . . . German men despised women. Why did they teach them anything at all?

The same impression, the sense of a half-impatient, half-exasperated tuition came to her from the lectures of Herr Winter and Herr Schraub.

Herr Winter, a thin tall withered-looking man with shabby hair and bony hands whose veins stood up in knots, drummed on the table as he taught botany and geography. The girls sat round bookless and politely attentive and seemed, the Germans at least, to remember all the facts for which he appealed during the last few minutes of his hour.  Miriam could never recall anything but his weary withered face.

Herr Schraub, the teacher of history, was, she felt, almost openly contemptuous of his class.  He would begin lecturing, almost before he was inside the door. He taught from a book, sitting with downcast eyes, his round red mass of face-- expressionless save for the bristling spikes of his tiny straw-coloured moustache and the rapid movements of his tight rounded little lips--persistently averted from his pupils.  For the last few minutes of his time he would, ironically, his eyes fixed ahead of him at a point on the table, snap questions--indicating his aim with a tapping finger, going round the table like a dealer at cards.  Surely the girls must detest him. . . . The Germans made no modification of their polite attentiveness.  Amongst the English only Gertrude and the Martins found any answers for him.  Miriam, proud of sixth-form history essays and the full marks she had generally claimed for them, had no memory for facts and dates; but she made up her mind that were she ever so prepared with a correct reply, nothing should drag from her any response to these military tappings.  Fraulein presided over these lectures from the corner of the sofa out of range of the eye of the teacher and horrified Miriam by voicelessly prompting the girls whenever she could.  There was no kind of preparation for these lessons.

2

Miriam mused over the difference between the bearing of these men and that of the masters she remembered and tried to find words.  What was it?  Had her masters been more--respectful than these Germans were?  She felt they had.  But it was not only that.  She recalled the men she remembered teaching week by week through all the years she had known them . . . the little bolster-like literature master, an albino, a friend of Browning, reading, reading to them as if it were worth while, as if they were equals . . . interested friends--that had never struck her at the time. . . . But it was true--she could not remember ever having felt a schoolgirl . . . or being "talked down" to . . . dear Stroodie, the music-master, and Monsieur--old whitehaired Monsieur, dearest of all, she could hear his gentle voice pleading with them on behalf of his treasures . . . the drilling-master with his keen, friendly blue eye . . . the briefless barrister who had taught them arithmetic in a baritone voice, laughing all the time but really wanting them to get on.

What was it she missed? Was it that her old teachers were "gentlemen" and these Germans were not? She pondered over this and came to the conclusion that the whole attitude of the Englishman and of Monsieur, her one Frenchman, towards her sex was different from that of these Germans. It occurred to her once in a flash during these puzzled musings that the lessons she had had at school would not have been given more zestfully, more as if it were worth while, had she and her schoolfellows been boys. Here she could not feel that. The teaching was grave enough. The masters felt the importance of what they taught . . . she felt that they were formal, reverently formal, "pompous" she called it, towards the facts that they flung out down the long schoolroom table, but that the relationship of their pupils to these facts seemed a matter of less indifference to them.

3

She began to recognise now with a glow of gratitude that her own teachers, those who were enthusiastic about their subjects--the albino, her dear Monsieur with his classic French prose, a young woman who had taught them logic and the beginning of psychology--that strange, new subject--were at least as enthusiastic about getting her and her mates awake and into relationship with something. They cared somehow.

She recalled the albino, his face and voice generally separated from his class by a book held vertically, close to his left eye, while he blocked the right eye with his free hand--his faintly wheezy tones bleating triumphantly out at the end of a passage from "The Ring and the Book," as he lowered his volume and bent beaming towards them all, his right eye still blocked, for response. Miss Donne, her skimpy skirt powdered with chalk, explaining a syllogism from the blackboard, turning quietly to them, her face all aglow, her chalky hands gently pressed together, "Do you *see?* Does anyone *see?*" Monsieur, spoiling them, sharpening their pencils, letting them cheat over their pages of rules, knowing quite well that each learned only one and directing his questioning accordingly, Monsieur dreaming over the things he read to them, repeating passages, wandering from his subject, making al-

lusions here and there--and all of them, she, at any rate, and Lilla--she knew, often-
-in paradise.  How rich and friendly and helpful they all seemed.

She began to wonder whether hers had been in some way a specially good
school.  Things had mattered there.  Somehow the girls had been made to feel they
mattered.  She remembered even old Stroodie--the least attached member of the
staff--asking her suddenly, once, in the middle of a music-lesson what she was going to do with her life and a day when the artistic vice-principal--who was a connection by marriage of Holman Hunt's and had met Ruskin, Miriam knew, several
times--had gone from girl to girl round the collected fifth and sixth forms asking
them each what they would best like to do in life.  Miriam had answered at once
with a conviction born that moment that she wanted to "write a book."  It irritated
her when she remembered during these reflections that she had not been able to
give to Fraulein Pfaff's public questioning any intelligible account of the school.
She might at least have told her of the connection with Ruskin and Browning and
Holman Hunt, whereas her muddled replies had led Fraulein to decide that her
school had been "a kind of high school."  She knew it had not been this.  She felt
there was something questionable about a high school.  She was beginning to think
that her school had been very good.  Pater had seen to that--that was one of the
things he had steered and seen to.  There had been a school they might have gone
to higher up the hill where one learned needlework even in the "first class" as they
called it instead of the sixth form as at her school, and "Calisthenics" instead of
drilling--and something called elocution--where the girls were "finished."  It was
an expensive school.  Had the teachers there taught the girls . . . as if they had no
minds?  Perhaps that school was more like the one she found herself in now?  She
wondered and wondered.  What was she going to do with her life after all these
years at the good school?  She began bit by bit to understand her agony on the day
of leaving.  It was there she belonged.  She ought to go back and go on.

One day she lay twisted and convulsed, face downwards on her bed at the
thought that she could never go back and begin.  If only she could really begin now,
knowing what she wanted. . . . She would talk now with those teachers. . . . Isn't it
all wonderful!  Aren't things wonderful!  Tell me some more. . . . She felt sure that
if she could go back, things would get clear.  She would talk and think and understand. . . . She did not linger over that.  It threatened a storm whose results would be

visible. She wondered what the other girls were doing--Lilla? She had heard nothing of her since that last term. She would write to her one day, perhaps. Perhaps not. . . . She would have to tell her that she was a governess. Lilla would think that very funny and would not care for her now that she was so old and worried. . . .

5

Woven through her retrospective appreciations came a doubt. She wondered whether, after all, her school had been right. Whether it ought to have treated them all so seriously. If she had gone to the other school she was sure she would never have heard of the Aesthetic Movement or felt troubled about the state of Ireland and India. Perhaps she would have grown up a Churchwoman . . . and "ladylike." Never.

She could only think that somehow she must be "different"; that a sprinkling of the girls collected in that school were different, too. The school she decided was new--modern--Ruskin. Most of the girls perhaps had not been affected by it. But some had. She had. The thought stirred her. She had. It was mysterious. Was it the school or herself? Herself to begin with. If she had been brought up differently, it could not, she felt sure, have made her very different--for long--nor taught her to be affable--to smile that smile she hated so. The school had done something to her. It had not gone against the things she found in herself. She wondered once or twice during these early weeks what she would have been like if she had been brought up with these German girls. What they were going to do with their lives was only too plain. All but Emma, she had been astounded to discover, had already a complete outfit of house-linen to which they were now adding fine embroideries and laces. All could cook. Minna had startled her one day by exclaiming with lit face, "Ach, ich koche so *schrecklich* gern!" Oh, I am so frightfully fond of cooking. . . . And they were placid and serene, secure in a kind of security Miriam had never met before. They did not seem to be in the least afraid of the future. She envied that. Their eyes and their hands were serene. . . . They would have houses and things they could do and understand, always. . . . How they must want to begin, she mused. . . . What a prison school must seem.

She thought of their comfortable German homes, of ruling and shopping and directing and being looked up to. . . . German husbands.

That thought she shirked.  Emma in particular she could not contemplate in relation to a German husband.

In any case one day these girls would be middle-aged . . . as Clara looked now . . . they would look like the German women on the boulevards and in the shops.

In the end she ceased to wonder that the German masters dealt out their wares to these girls so superciliously.

And yet . . . German music, a line of German poetry, a sudden light on Clara's face. . . .

6

There was one other teacher, a Swiss and some sort of minister she supposed as everyone called him the Herr Pastor.  She wondered whether he was in any sense the spiritual adviser of the school and regarded him with provisional suspicion.  She had seen him once, sitting short and very black and white at the head of the school-room table.  His black beard and dark eyes as he sat with his back to the window made his face gleam like a mask.  He had spoken very rapidly as he told the girls the life-story of some poet.

7

The time that was not taken up by the masters and the regular succession of rich and savoury meals--wastefully plentiful they seemed to Miriam--was filled in by Fraulein Pfaff with occupations devised apparently from hour to hour.  On a master's morning the girls collected in the schoolroom one by one as they finished their bed-making and dusting.  On other days the time immediately after break-fast was full of uncertainty and surmise.  Judging from the interchange between the four first-floor bedrooms whose doors were always open during this bustling interval, Miriam, listening apprehensively as she did her share of work on the top floor, gathered that the lack of any planned programme was a standing annoyance to the English girls.  Millie, still imperfectly acclimatised, carrying out her duties in a large bibbed apron, was plaintive about it in her conscientious German nearly every morning. The Martins, when the sense of Fraulein as providence was strong upon them made their beds vindictively, rapping out sarcasms to be alternately mocked and giggled at by Jimmie who was generally heard, as the gusts subsided, dispensing the comforting assurance that it wouldn't last for ever. Miriam once heard even Judy grumbling to herself in a mumbling undertone as she carried the lower landing's collective "wasche" upstairs to the back attic to await the quarterly waschfrau.

The German side of the landing was uncritical. On free mornings the Germans had one preoccupation. It was generally betrayed by Emma in a loud excited whisper, aimed across the landing: "Gehen wir zu Kreipe? Do we go to Kreipe's?" "Kreipe, Kreipe," Minna and Clara would chorus devoutly from their respective rooms. Gertrude on these occasions always had an air of knowledge and would sometimes prophesy. To what extent Fraulein did confide in the girl and how much was due to her experience of the elder woman's habit of mind Miriam could never determine. But her prophecies were always fulfilled.

Fraulein, who generally went to the basement kitchen from the breakfast-table, would be heard on the landing towards the end of the busy half-hour, rallying and criticising the housemaids in her gentle caustic voice. She never came to the top floor. Miriam and Mademoiselle, who agreed in accomplishing their duties with great despatch and spending any spare time sitting in their jackets on their respective beds reading or talking, would listen for her departure. There was always a moment when they knew that the excitement was over and the landing stricken into certainty. Then Mademoiselle would flit to the top of the stairs and demand, leaning over the balustrade, "Eh bien! Eh bien!" and someone would retail directions.

Sometimes Anna would appear in her short, chequered cotton dress, shawled and with her market basket on her arm, and would summon Gertrude alone or with Solomon Martin to Fraulein's room opposite the saal on the ground floor. The appearance of Anna was the signal for bounding anticipations. It nearly always meant a holiday and an expedition.

8

During the cold weeks after Miriam's arrival there were no expeditions; and very commonly uncertainty was prolonged by a provisional distribution of the ten girls between the kitchen and the five pianos. In this case neither she nor Mademoiselle received any instructions. Mademoiselle would go to the saal with needle-work, generally the lighter household mending. The saal piano at practising time was allotted to the pupil to whom the next music lesson was due, and Mademoiselle spent the greater part of her time installed, either awaiting the possible arrival of Herr Bossenberger or presiding over his lessons when he came. Miriam, unprovided for, sitting in the schoolroom with a book, awaiting events, would watch her disappear unconcernedly through the folding doors, every time with fresh wonder. She did not want to take her place, though it would have meant listening to Herr Bossenberger's teaching and a quiet alcove of freedom from the apprehensive uncertainty that hung over so many of her hours. It seemed to her odd, not quite the thing, to have a third person in the room at a music lesson. She tried to imagine a lesson being given to herself under these conditions. The thought was abhorrent. And Mademoiselle, of all people. Miriam could see her sitting in the saal, wrapped in all the coolness of her complete insensibility to music, her eyes bent on her work, the quick movements of her small, thin hands, the darting gleam of her thimble, the dry way she had of clearing her throat, a gesture that was an accentuation of the slightly metallic quality of her voice, and expressed, for Miriam, in sound, that curious sense of circumspect frugality she was growing to realise as characteristic of Mademoiselle's face in repose.

The saal doors closed, the little door leading into the hall became the centre of Miriam's attention. Before long, sometimes at the end of ten minutes, this door would open and the day become eventful. She had already taken Clara, with Emma, to make a third, three times to her masseuse, sitting for half an hour in a room above a chemist's shop so stuffy beyond anything in her experience that she had carried away nothing but the sense of its closely-interwoven odours, a dim picture of Clara in a saffron-coloured wrapper and the shocked impression of the resounding thwackings undergone by her. Emma was paying a series of visits to the dentist and might appear at the schoolroom door with frightened eyes, holding it open--"Hendchen! Ich muss zum Zahnarzt." Miriam dreaded these excursions. The first time Miriam had accompanied her Emma had had "gas." Miriam, assailed by a loud scream followed by the peremptory voices of two white-coated, fiercely moustached operators, one of whom seemed to be holding Emma in the chair, had started from her sofa in the background. "Brutes!" she had declared and reached the chair-side voluble in unintelligible German to find Emma serenely emerging from unconsciousness. Once she had taken Gertrude to the dentist--another dentist, an elderly man, practising in a frock-coat in a heavily-furnished room with high sash windows, the lower sashes filled with stained glass. There had been a driving March wind and Gertrude with a shawl round her face had battled gallantly along shouting through her shawl. Miriam had made out nothing clearly, but the fact that the dentist's wife had a title in her own right. Gertrude had gone through her trial, prolonged by some slight complication, without an anesthetic, in alternations of tense silence and great gusts of her hacking laughter. Miriam, sitting strained in the far background near a screen covered with a mass of strange embroideries, wondered how she really felt. That, she realised with a vision of Gertrude going on through life in smart costumes, one would never know.

9

The thing Miriam dreaded most acutely was a visit with Minna to her aurist. She learned with horror that Minna was obliged every few months to submit to a series of small operations at the hands of the tall, scholarly-looking man, with large, clear, impersonal eyes, who carried on his practice high up in a great block of buildings in a small faded room with coarse coffee-coloured curtains at its smudgy windows. The character of his surroundings added a great deal to her abhorrence of his attentions to Minna.

The room was densely saturated with an odour which she guessed to be that of stale cigar-smoke. It seemed so tangible in the room that she looked about at first for visible signs of its presence. It was like an invisible fog and seemed to affect her breathing.

Coming and going upon the dense staleness of the room and pervading the immediate premises was a strange savoury pungency.  Miriam could not at first identify it.  But as the visits multiplied and she noticed the same odour standing in faint patches here and there about the stairways and corridors of the block, it dawned upon her that it must be onions--onions freshly frying but with a quality of accumulated richness that she could not explain.  But the fact of the dominating kitchen side by side with the consulting-room made her speculate.  She imagined the doctor's wife, probably in that kitchen, a hard-browed bony North German woman.  She saw the clear-eyed man at his meals; and imagined his slippers.  There were dingy books in the room where Minna started and moaned.

She compared this entourage with her recollection of her one visit to an oculist in Harley Street.  His stately house, the exquisite freshness of his appointments and his person stood out now.  The English she assured herself were more refined than the Germans.  Even the local doctor at Barnes whose effect upon her mother's perpetual ill-health, upon Eve's nerves and Sarah's mysterious indigestion was so impermanent that the very sound of his name exasperated her, had something about him that she failed entirely to find in this German--something she could respect.  She wondered whether the professional classes in Germany were all like this specialist and living in this way.  Minna's parents she knew were paying large fees.

## 10

These dreaded expeditions brought a compensation.

Her liking for Minna grew with each visit.  She wondered at her.  Here she was with her nose and her ear--she was subject to rheumatism too--it would always, Miriam reflected, be doctor's treatment for her.  She wondered at her perpetual cheerfulness.  She saw her with a pang of pity, going through life with her illnesses, capped in defiance of all the care she bestowed on her person, with her disconcerting nose, a nose she reflected, that would do splendidly for charades.

## 11

On several occasions a little contingent selected from the pianos and kitchen had appeared in the schoolroom and settled down to read German with Fraulein.

Miriam had been despatched to a piano. After these readings the mid-morning lunching-plates of sweet custard-like soup or chocolate soup or perhaps glasses of sweet syrup and biscuits--were, if Fraulein were safely out of earshot, voluble indignation meetings. If she were known to be in the room beyond the little schoolroom, lunch was taken in silence except for Gertrude's sallies, cheerful generalisations from Minna or Jimmie, and grudging murmurs of response.

On the mornings of Fraulein's German readings the school never went to Kreipe's. Going to Kreipe's Miriam perceived was a sign of fair weather.

They had been twice since her coming. Sitting at a little marble-topped table with the Bergmanns near the window and overlooking the full flood of the Georgstrasse Miriam felt a keen renewal of the sense of being abroad. Here she sat, in the little enclosure of this upper room above a shopful of strange Delikatessen, securely adrift. Behind her she felt, not home but the German school where she belonged. Here they all sat, free. Germany was all around them. They were in the midst of it. Fraulein Pfaff seemed far away. . . . How strange of her to send them there. . . . She glanced towards the two tables of English girls in the centre of the room wondering whether they felt as she did. . . . They had come to Germany. They were sharing it with her. It must be changing them. They must be different for having come. They would all go back she supposed. But they would not be the same as those who had never come. She was sure they felt something of this. They were sitting about in easy attitudes. How English they all looked . . . for a moment she wanted to go and sit with them--just sit with them, rejoice in being abroad; in having got away. She imagined all their people looking in and seeing them so thoroughly at home in this little German restaurant free from home influences, in a little world of their own. She felt a pang of response as she heard their confidently raised voices. She could see they were all, even Judy, a little excited. They chaffed each other.

Gertrude had taken everyone's choice between coffee and chocolate and given an order.

Orders for schocolade were heard from all over the room. There were only women there--wonderful German women in twos and threes--ladies out shopping, Miriam supposed. She managed intermittently to watch three or four of them and wondered what kind of conversation made them so emphatic--whether it was because they held themselves so well and "spoke out" that everything they said seemed so important.  She had never seen women with so much decision in their bearing.  She found herself drawing herself up.

She heard German laughter about the room.  The sounds excited her and she watched eagerly for laughing faces. . . . They were different. . . . The laughter sounded differently and the laughing faces were different.  The eyes were expressionless as they laughed--or evil . . . they had that same knowing way of laughing as though everything were settled--but they did not pretend to be refined as Englishwomen did . . . they had the same horridness . . . but they were . . . jolly. . . . They could shout if they liked.

Three cups of thick-looking chocolate, each supporting a little hillock of solid cream arrived at her table.  Clara ordered cakes.

At the first sip, taken with lips that slid helplessly on the surprisingly thick rim of her cup Miriam renounced all the beverages she had ever known as unworthy.

She chose a familiar-looking eclair--Clara and Emma ate cakes that seemed to be alternate slices of cream and very spongy coffee-coloured cake and then followed Emma's lead with an open tartlet on which plump green gooseberries stood in a thick brown syrup.


12


During dinner Fraulein Pfaff went the round of the table with questions as to what had been consumed at Kreipe's.  The whole of the table on her right confessed to one Kuchen with their chocolate.  In each case she smiled gravely and required the cake to be described.  The meaning of the pilgrimage of enquiry came to Miriam when Fraulein reached Gertrude and beamed affectionately in response to her careless "Schokolade und ein Biskuit."  Miriam and the Bergmanns were alone in their excesses.


13


Even walks were incalculable excepting on Saturdays, when at noon Anna turned out the schoolrooms.  Then--unless to Miriam's great satisfaction it rained and they had a little festival shut in in holiday mood in the saal, the girls playing and singing, Anna loudly obliterating the week-days next door and the secure harbour of Sunday ahead--they went methodically out and promenaded the streets of Hanover for an hour. These Saturday walks were a recurring humiliation. If they had occurred daily, some crisis, she felt sure would have arisen for her.

The little party would file out under the leadership of Gertrude--Fraulein Pfaff smiling parting directions adjuring them to come back safe and happy to the beehive and stabbing at them all the while, Miriam felt, with her keen eye--through the high doorway that pierced the high wall and then--charge down the street. Gertrude alone, having been in Hanover and under Fraulein Pfaff's care since her ninth year, was instructed as to the detail of their tour and she swung striding on ahead, the ends of her long fur boa flying out in the March wind, making a flourishing scrollwork round her hounding tailor-clad form--the Martins, short-skirted and thick-booted, with hard cloth jackets and hard felt hats, and short thick pelerines almost running on either side, Jimmie, Millie and Judy hard behind. Miriam's ever-recurring joyous sense of emergence and her longing to go leisurely and alone along these wonderful streets, to go on and on at first and presently to look, had to give way to the necessity of keeping Gertrude and her companions in sight. On they went relentlessly through the Saturday throng along the great Georgstrasse--a foreign paradise, with its great bright cafes and the strange promising detail of its shops--tantalisingly half seen.

She hated, too, the discomfort of walking thus at this pace through streets along pavements in her winter clothes. They hampered her horribly. Her heavy three-quarter length coat made her too warm and bumped against her as she hurried along--the little fur pelerine which redeemed its plainness tickled her neck and she felt the outline of her stiff hat like a board against her uneasy forehead. Her inflexible boots soon tired her. . . . But these things she could have endured. They were not the main source of her trouble. She could have renounced the delights all round her, made terms with the discomforts and looked for alleviations. But it was during these walks that she began to perceive that she was making, in a way she had not at all anticipated, a complete failure of her rôle of English teacher. The three weeks' haphazard curriculum had brought only one repetition of her English lesson in the smaller schoolroom; and excepting at meals, when whatever conversation there was was general and polyglot, she was never, in the house, alone with her

German pupils. The cessation of the fixed readings arranged with her that first day by Fraulein Pfaff did not, in face of the general absence of method, at all disturb her. Mademoiselle's classes had, she discovered, except for the weekly mending, long since lapsed altogether. These walks, she soon realised, were supposed to be her and her pupils' opportunity. No doubt Fraulein Pfaff believed that they represented so many hours of English conversation--and they did not. It was cheating, pure and simple. She thought of fee-paying parents, of the probable prospectus. "French and English governesses."

14

Her growing conviction and the distress of it were confirmed each week by a spectacle she could not escape and was rapidly growing to hate. Just in front of her and considerably behind the flying van, her full wincey skirt billowing out beneath what seemed to Miriam a dreadfully thin little close-fitting stockinette jacket, trotted Mademoiselle--one hand to the plain brim of her large French hat, and obviously conversational with either Minna and Elsa or Clara and Emma on either side of her. Generally it was Minna and Elsa, Minna brisk and trim and decorous as to her neat plaid skirt, however hurried, and Elsa showing her distress by the frequent twisting of one or other of her ankles which looked, to Miriam, like sticks above her high-heeled shoes. Mademoiselle's broad hat-brim flapped as her head turned from one companion to the other. Sometimes Miriam caught the mocking tinkle of her laughter. That all three were interested, too, Miriam gathered from the fact that they could not always be relied upon to follow Gertrude. The little party had returned one day in two separate groups, fortunately meeting before the Waldstrasse gate was reached, owing to Mademoiselle's failure to keep Gertrude in sight. There was no doubt, too, that the medium of their intercourse was French, for Mademoiselle's knowledge of German had not, for all her six months at the school, got beyond a few simple and badly managed words and phrases. Miriam felt that this French girl was perfectly carrying out Fraulein Pfaff's design. She talked to her pupils, made them talk; the girls were amused and happy and were picking up French. It was admirable and it was wonderful to Miriam because she felt quite sure that Mademoiselle had no clear idea in her own mind that she was carrying out any design at all. That irritated Miriam. Mademoiselle liked talking to her girls. Miriam was beginning to know that she did not want to talk to her girls. Almost from the first she had begun to know it. She felt sure that if Fraulein Pfaff had been invisibly present at any one of her solitary conversational encounters with these German girls she would have been judged and condemned. Elsa Speier had been the worst. Miriam could see as she thought of her, the angle of the high garden wall of a corner house in Waldstrasse and above it a blossoming almond tree. "How lovely that tree is," she had said. She remembered trying hard to talk and to make her talk and making no impression upon the girl. She remembered monosyllables and the pallid averted face and Elsa's dreadful ankles. She had walked along intent and indifferent and presently she had felt a sort of irritation rise through her struggling. And then further on in the walk, she could not remember how it had arisen, there was a moment when Elsa had said with unmoved, averted face hurriedly, "My fazzer is offitser"--and it seemed to Miriam as if this were the answer to everything she had tried to say, to her remark about the almond-tree and everything else; and then she felt that there was nothing more to be said between them. They were both quite silent. Everything seemed settled. Miriam's mind called up a picture of a middle-aged man in a Saxon blue uniform--all voice and no brains--and going to take to gardening in his old age--and longed to tell Elsa of her contempt for all military men. Clearly she felt Elsa's and Elsa's mother's feeling towards herself. Elsa's mother had thin ankles, too, and was like Elsa intent and cold and dead. She could imagine Elsa in society now--hard and thin and glittery--she would be stylish--military men's women always were. The girl had avoided being with her during walks since then, and they never voluntarily addressed one another. Minna and the Bergmanns had talked to her. Minna responded to everything she said in her eager husky voice--not because she was interested Miriam felt, but because she was polite, and it had tired her once or twice dreadfully to go on "making conversation" with Minna. She had wanted to like being with these three. She felt she could give them something. It made her full of solicitude to glance at either of them at her side. She had longed to feel at home with them and to teach them things worth teaching; they seemed pitiful in some way, like children in her hands. She did not know how to begin. All her efforts and their efforts left them just as pitiful.

## 15

Each occasion left her more puzzled and helpless. Now and again she thought there was going to he a change. She would feel a stirring of animation in her companions. Then she would discover that someone was being discussed, generally one of the girls; or perhaps they were beginning to tell her something about Fraulein Pfaff, or talking about food. These topics made her feel ill at ease at once. Things were going wrong. It was not to discuss such things that they were together out in the air in the wonderful streets and boulevards of Hanover. She would grow cold and constrained, and the conversation would drop.

And then, suddenly, within a day or so of each other, dreadful things had happened.

The first had come on the second occasion of her going with Minna to see Dr. Dieckel. Minna, as they were walking quietly along together had suddenly begun in a broken English which soon turned to shy, fluent, animated German, to tell about a friend, an *apotheker,* a man, Miriam gathered--missing many links in her amazement--in a shop, the chemist's shop where her parents dealt, in the little country town in Pomerania which was her home. Minna was so altered, looked so radiantly happy whilst she talked about this man that Miriam had wanted to put out a hand and touch her. Afterwards she could recall the sound of her voice as it was at that moment with its yearning and its promise and its absolute confidence. Minna was so certain of her happiness--at the end of each hurried little phrase her voice sounded like a chord--like three strings sounding at once on some strange instrument.

And soon afterwards Emma had told her very gravely, with Clara walking a little aloof, her doglike eyes shining as she gazed into the distance, of a "most beautiful man" with a brown moustache, with whom Clara was in love. He was there in the town, in Hanover, a hair-specialist, treating Clara's thin short hair.

## 16

Even Emma had a "jungling." He had a very vulgar surname, too vulgar to be spoken; it was breathed against Miriam's shoulder in the half-light.  Miriam was begged to forget it at once and to remember only the beautiful little name that preceded it.

At the time she had timidly responded to all these stories and had felt glad that the confidences had come to her.

Mademoiselle, she knew, had never received them.

But after these confidences there were no more serious attempts at general conversation.

## 17

Miriam felt ashamed of her share in the hairdresser and the chemist.  Emma's jungling might possibly be a student. . . . She grieved over the things that she felt were lying neglected, "things in general" she felt sure she ought to discuss with the girls . . . improving the world . . . leaving it better than you found it . . . the importance of life . . . sleeping and dreaming that life was beauty and waking and finding it was duty . . . making things better, reforming . . . being a reformer. . . . Pater always said young people always wanted to reform the universe . . . perhaps it was so . . . and nothing could be done.  Clearly she was not the one to do anything.  She could do nothing even with these girls and she was nearly eighteen.

Once or twice she wondered whether they ever had thoughts about things . . . she felt they must; if only she were not shy, if she had a different manner, she would find out.  She knew she despised them as they were.  She could do nothing.  Her fine ideas were no good.  She did less than silly little Mademoiselle.  And all the time Fraulein thinking she was talking and influencing them was keeping her . . . in Germany.

# CHAPTER VI

## 1

Fraulein Pfaff came to the breakfast-table a little late in a grey stuff dress with a cream-coloured ruching about the collar-band and ruchings against her long brown wrists. The girls were already in their places, and as soon as grace was said she began talking in a gentle decisive voice.

"Martins' sponge-bags"--her face creased for her cavernous smile--"are both large and strong--beautiful gummi-bags, each large enough to contain a family of sponges."

The table listened intently. Miriam tried to remember the condition of her side of the garret. She saw Judy's scarlet flush across the table.

"Millie," went on Fraulein, "is the owner of a damp-proof hold-all for the bath which is a veritable monument."

"Monument?" laughed a German voice apprehensively.

"Fancy a monument on your washstand," tittered Jimmie.

Fraulein raised her voice slightly, still smiling. Miriam heard her own name and stiffened. "Miss Henderson is an Englishwoman too--and our little Ulrica joins the English party." Fraulein's voice had thickened and grown caressing. Perhaps no one was in trouble. Ulrica bowed. Her wide-open startled eyes and the out-line of her pale face remained unchanged. Still gentle and tender-voiced Fraulein reached Judy and the Germans. All was well. Soaps and sponges could go in the English bags. Judy's downcast crimson face began to recover its normal clear flush, and the Germans joined in the general rejoicing. They were to go, Miriam gathered, in the afternoon to the baths. . . . She had never been to a public baths. . . . She wished Fraulein could know there were two bathrooms in the house at Barnes, and then wondered whether in German baths one was left to oneself or whether there, too, there would be some woman superintending.

Fraulein jested softly on about her children and their bath. Gertrude and Jimmie recalled incidents of former bathings--the stories went on until breakfast had prolonged itself into a sitting of happy adventurers. The room was very warm, and coffee-scented. Clara at her corner sat with an outstretched arm nearly touching Fraulein Pfaff who was sitting forward glowing and shedding the light of her dark young eyes on each in turn. There were many elbows on the table. Judy's head was raised and easy. Miriam noticed that the whiteness of her neck was whiter than those strange bright patches where her eyelashes shone. Ulrica's eyes went from face to face as she listened and Miriam fed upon the outlines of her head.

She wished she could place her hands on either side of its slenderness and feel the delicate skull and gaze undisturbed into the eyes.

2

Fraulein Pfaff rose at last from the table.

"Na, Kinder," she smiled, holding her arms out to them all.

She turned to the nearest window.

"Die Fenster auf!" she cried, in quivering tones, "Die Herzen auf!" "Up with windows! Up with hearts!"

Her hands struggled with the hasp of the long-closed outer frame. The girls crowded round as the lattices swung wide. The air poured in.

Miriam stood in a vague crowd seeing nothing. She felt the movement of her own breathing and the cool streaming of the air through her nostrils. She felt comely and strong.

"That's a thrush," she heard Bertha Martin say as a chattering flew across a distant garden--and Fraulein's half-singing reply, "Know you, children, what the thrush says? Know you?" and Minna's eager voice sounding out into the open, "D'ja, d'ja, ich, weiss--Ritzifizier, sagt sie, Ritzifizier, das vierundzwanzigste Jahr!" and voices imitating.

"Spring! Spring! Spring!" breathed Clara, in a low sing-song.

Miriam found herself with her hands on the doors leading into the saal, pushing them gently. Why not? Everything had changed. Everything was good. The great doors gave, the sunlight streamed from behind her into the quiet saal. She went along the pathway it made and stood in the middle of the room. The voices from the schoolroom came softly, far away. She went to the centre window and pushing aside its heavy curtains saw for the first time that it had no second pane like the others, but led directly into a sort of summer-house, open in front and leading by a wooden stairway down to the garden plot. Up the railing of the stairway and over the entrance of the summer-house a creeping plant was putting out tiny leaves. It was in shadow, but the sun caught the sharply peaked gable of the summer-house and on the left, the tops of the high shrubs lining the pathway leading to the wooden door and the great balls finishing the high stone gateway shone yellow with sunlit lichen. She heard the schoolroom windows close and the girls clearing away the breakfast things and escaped upstairs singing.

Before she had finished her duties a summons came. Jimmie brought the message, panting as she reached the top of the stairs.

"Hurry up, Hendy!" she gasped. "You're one of the distinguished ones, my dear!"

"What do you mean?" Miriam began apprehensively as she turned to go. "Oh, Jimmie----" she tried to laugh ingratiatingly. "*Do* tell me what you mean?" Jimmie turned and raised a plump hand with a sharply-quirked little finger and a dangle of lace-edged handkerchief.

"You're a *swell,* my dear. You're in with the specials and the classic knot."

"What do you mean?"

"You're going to read--Gerty, or something--no idiots admitted. You're going it, Hendy. Ta-ta. Fly! Don't stick in the mud, old slowcoach."

"I'll come in a second," said Miriam, adjusting hairpins.

She was to read Goethe . . . with Fraulein Pfaff. . . . Fraulein knew she would be one of the few who would do for a Goethe reading. She reached the little room smiling with happiness.

"Here she is," was Fraulein's greeting. The little group--Ulrica, Minna and Solomon Martin were sitting about informally in the sunlit window space, Minna and Solomon had needlework--Ulrica was gazing out into the garden. Miriam sank into the remaining low-seated wicker chair and gave herself up. Fraulein began to read, as she did at prayers, slowly, almost below her breath, but so clearly that Miriam could distinguish each word and her face shone as she bent over her book. It was a poem in blank verse with long undulating lines. Miriam paid no heed to the sense. She heard nothing but the even swing, the slight rising and falling of the clear low tones. She felt once more the opening of the schoolroom window--she saw the little brown summer-house and the sun shining on the woodwork of its porch. Summer coming. Summer coming in Germany. She drew a long breath. The poem was telling of someone getting away out of a room, out of "narrow conversation" to a meadow-covered plain--of a white pathway winding through the green.

Minna put down her sewing and turned her kind blue eyes to Fraulein Pfaff's face.

Ulrica sat drooping, her head bent, her great eyes veiled, her hands entwined on her lap. . . . The little pathway led to a wood. The wide landscape disappeared. Fraulein's voice ceased.

3

She handed the book to Ulrica, indicating the place and Ulrica read. Her voice sounded a higher pitch than Fraulein's. It sounded out rich and full and liquid, and seemed to shake her slight body and echo against the walls of her face. It filled the room with a despairing ululation. Fraulein seemed by contrast to have been whispering piously in a corner.

Listening to the beseeching tones, hearing no words, Miriam wished that the eyes could be raised, when the reading ceased, to hers and that she could go and put her hands about the beautiful head, scarcely touching it and say, "It is all right. I will stay with you always."

She watched the little hand that was not engaged with the book and lay abandoned, outstretched, listless and shining on her knee. Solomon's needle snapped. She frowned and roused herself heavily to secure another from the basket on the floor at her side. Miriam, flashing hatred at her, caught Fraulein's fascinating gaze fixed on Ulrica; and saw it hastily turn to an indulgent smile as the eyes became conscious, moving for a moment without reaching her in the direction of her own low chair. A tap came at the door and Anna's flat tones, like a voluble mechanical doll, announced a postal official waiting in the hall for Ulrica--with a package. "Ein Packet . . . a-a-ach," wailed Ulrica, rising, her hands trembling, her great eyes radiant. Fraulein sent her off with Solomon to superintend the signing and payments and give help with the unpacking.

"The little heiress," she said devoutly, with her wide smile as she returned from the door.

"Oh . . ." said Miriam politely.

"Sie, nun, Miss Henderson," concluded Fraulein, handing her the book and indicating the passage Ulrica had just read. "Nun, Sie," she repeated brightly, and Minna drew her chair a little nearer making a small group.

4

"Schiller" she saw at the top of the page and the title of the poem "Der Spaziergang." Miriam laid the book on the end of her knee, and leaning over it, read nervously. Her tones reassured her. She noticed that she read very slowly, breaking up the rhythm into sentences--and authoritatively as if she were recounting an experience of her own. She knew at first that she was reading like a cultured person and that Fraulein would recognise this at once, she knew that the perfect assurance of her pronunciation would make it seem that she understood every word, but soon these feelings gave way to the sense half grasped of the serpentine path winding and mounting through a wood, of a glimpse of a distant valley, of flocks and villages, and of her unity with Fraulein and Minna seeing and feeling all these things together. She finished the passage--Fraulein quietly commended her reading and Minna said something about her earnestness.

"Miss Henderson is always a little earnest," said Fraulein affectionately.

5

"Are you dressed, Hendy?"

Miriam, who had sat up in her bath when the drumming came at the door, answered sleepily, "No, I shan't be a minute."

"Don't you want to see the diving?"

All Jimmie's fingers seemed to be playing exercises against the panels. Miriam wished she would restrain them and leave her alone. She did not in the least wish to see the diving.

"I shan't be a minute," she shouted crossly, and let her shoulders sink once more under the comforting water. It was the first warm water she had encountered since that night when Mademoiselle had carried the jugs upstairs. Her soap, so characterless in the chilly morning basin lathered freely in the warmth and was fragrant in the steamy air. When Jimmie's knocking came she was dreaming blissfully of baths with Harriett--the dissipated baths of the last six months between tea and dinner with a theatre or a dance ahead. Harriett, her hair strained tightly into a white crocheted net, her snub face shining through the thick steam, tubbing and jesting at the wide end of the huge porcelain bath, herself at the narrow end commanding the taps under the steam-dimmed beams of the red-globed gasjets . . . sponge-fights . . . and those wonderful summer bathings when they had come in from long tennis-playing in the sun, filled the bath with cold water and sat in the silence of broad daylight immersed to the neck, confronting each other.

Seeing no sign of anything she could recognise as a towel, she pulled at a huge drapery hanging like a counterpane in front of a coil of pipes extending half-way to the ceiling. The pipes were too hot to touch and the heavy drapery was more than warm and obviously meant for drying purposes. Sitting wrapped in its folds, dizzy and oppressed, she longed for the flourish of a rough towel and a window open at the top. She could see no ventilation of any kind in her white cell. By the time her heavy outdoor things were on she was faint with exhaustion, and hurried down the corridor towards the shouts and splashings echoing in the great, open, glass-roofed swimming-bath. She was just in time to see a figure in scarlet and white, standing out on the high gallery at the end of a projecting board which broke the little white balustrade, throw up its arms and leap out and flash--its joined hands pointed downwards towards the water, its white feet sweeping up like the tail of a swooping bird--cleave the green water and disappear. The huge bath was empty of bathers and smoothly rippling save where the flying body had cleaved it and left wavelets and bubbles. The girls--most of them in their outdoor things--were gathered in a little group near the marble steps leading down into the water farthest from where the diver had dropped, stirring and exclaiming. As Miriam was approaching them a red-capped head came cleanly up out of the water near the steps and she recognised the strong jaw and gleaming teeth of Gertrude. She neither spluttered nor shook her head. Her eyes were wide and smiling, and her raucous laugh rang out above the applause of the group of girls.

Miriam paused under the overhanging gallery. Her eyes went, incredulously, up to the spring-board. It seemed impossible . . . and all that distance above the water. . . . Her gaze was drawn to the flicking of the curtain of one of the little compartments lining the gallery.

6

"Hullo, Hendy, let me get into my cubicle." Gertrude stood before her dripping and smiling.

"However on earth did you do it?" said Miriam, gazing incredulously at the ruddy wet face.

Gertrude's smile broadened. "Go on," she said, shaking the drops from her chin, "it's all in the day's work."

In the hard clear light Miriam saw that the teeth that looked so gleaming and strong in the distance were slightly ribbed and fluted and had serrated edges. Large stoppings showed like shadows behind the thin shells of the upper front ones. Even Gertrude might be ill one day; but she would never be ill and sad and helpless. That was clear from the neat way she plunged in through her curtains. . . .

Miriam's eyes went back to the row of little curtained recesses in the gallery. The drapery that had flapped was now half withdrawn, the light from the glass roof fell upon the top of a head flung back and shaking its mane of hair. The profile was invisible, but the sheeny hair rippled in thick gilded waves almost to the floor. . . . How hateful of her, thought Miriam. . . . How beautiful. I should be just the same if I had hair like that . . . that's Germany. . . . Lohengrin. . . . She stood adoring. "Stay and talk while I get on my togs," came Gertrude's voice from behind her curtains.

Miriam glanced towards the marble steps. The little group had disappeared. She turned helplessly towards Gertrude's curtains. She could not think of anything to say to her. She was filled with apprehension. "I wonder what we shall do to-morrow," she presently murmured.

"I don't," gasped Gertrude, towelling.

Miriam waited for the prophecy.

"Old Lahmann's back from Geneva," came the harsh panting voice.

"Pastor Lahmann?" repeated Miriam.

"None other, Madame."

"Have you seen him?" went on Miriam dimly, wishing that she might be released.

"Scots wha hae, no! But I saw Lily's frills."

The billows of gold hair in the gallery were being piled up by two little hands--white and plump like Eve's, but with quick clever irritating movements, and a thin sweet self-conscious voice began singing "Du, meine *Seele*." Miriam lost interest in the vision. . . . They were all the same. Men liked creatures like that. She could imagine that girl married.

"Lily and his wife were great friends," Gertrude was saying. "She's dead, you know."

"*Is* she," said Miriam emphatically.

"She used to be always coming when I first came over, Scots wha--blow--got a pin, Hendy? We shan't have his . . . thanks, you're a saint . . . his boys in the school-room any more now."

"Are those Pastor Lahmann's boys?" said Miriam, noticing Gertrude's hair was coarse, each hair a separate thread. "She's the wiry plucky kind. How she must despise me," said her mind.

"Well," said Gertrude, switching back her curtain to lace her boots. "Long may Lily beam. I like summer weather myself."

Miriam turned away. Gertrude half-dressed behind the curtains was too clever for her. She could not face her unveiled with vacant eyes.

"The summer is jolly, isn't it?" she said uneasily.

"You're right, my friend. Hullo! There's Emmchen looking for you. I expect the Germans have just finished their annual. They never come into the Schwimmbad, they're always too late. I should think you'd better toddle them home, Hendy--the darlings might catch cold."

"Don't we all go together?"

"We go as we are ready, from this establishment, just anyhow as long as we're not in ones or twos--Lily won't have twos, as I dare say you've observed.  Be good, my che-hild," she said heartily, drawing on her second boot, "and you'll be happy--sehr sehr happy, I hope, Hendy."

7

"Thank you," laughed Miriam.  Emma's hands were on her muff, stroking it eagerly.  "Hendchen, Hendchen," she cooed in her consoling tones, "to house to house, I am so angry--hangry."

"Hungry."

"Hungry, yes, and Minna and Clara is ready.  Kom!"

The child linked arms with her and pulled Miriam towards the corridor.  Once out of sight under the gallery she slipped her arm round Miriam's waist.  "Oh, Hendchen, my darling beautiful, you have so lovely teint after your badth--oh, I am zo hangry, oh Hendchen, I luff you zo, I am zo haypie, kiss me one small, small kiss."

"What a baby you are," said Miriam, half turning as the girl's warm lips brushed the angle of her jaw.  "Yes, we'll go home, come along."

The corridor was almost airless.  She longed to get out into the open.  They found Minna at a table in the entrance hall her head propped on her hand, snoring gently.  Clara sat near her with closed eyes.

As the little party of four making its way home, cleansed and hungry, united and happy, stood for a moment on a tree-planted island half-way across a wide open space, Minna with her eager smile said, gazing, "Oh, I would like a glass Bier."  Miriam saw very distinctly the clear sunlight on the boles of the trees showing every ridge and shade of colour as it had done on the peaked summer-house porch in the morning.  The girls closed in on her during the moment of disgust which postponed her response.

"Dear Hendchen!  We are alone!  Just we nice four!  Just only one most little small glass!  Just one!  Kind best, Hendchen!" she heard.  She pushed her way through the little group pretending to ignore their pleadings and to look for obstacles to their passage to the opposite curb.  She felt her disgust was absurd and was asking herself why the girls should not have their beer.  She would like to watch them, she knew; these little German Fraus-to-be serenely happy at their bier table on this bright afternoon. They closed in on her again. Emma in the gutter in front of her. She felt arms and hands, and the pleading voices besieged her again. Emma's upturned tragic face, her usually motionless lips a beseeching tunnel, her chin and throat moving to her ardent words made Miriam laugh. It *was* disgusting. "No, no," she said hastily, backing away from them to the end of the island. "Of course not. Come along. Don't be silly." The elder girls gave in. Emma kept up a little solo of reproach hanging on Miriam's arm. "Very strict. Cold English. No bier. I want to home. I have bier to home" until they were in sight of the high walls of Waldstrasse.

8

Pastor Lahmann gave a French lesson the next afternoon.
"Sur l'eau, si beau!"
This refrain threatening for the third time, three or four of the girls led by Bertha Martin, supplied it in a subdued singsong without waiting for Pastor Lahmann's slow voice. Miriam had scarcely attended to his discourse. He had begun in flat easy tones, describing his visit to Geneva, the snowclad mountains, the quiet lake, the spring flowers. His words brought her no vision and her mind wandered, half tethered. But when he began reading the poem she sank into the rhythm and turned towards him and fixed expectant eyes upon his face. His expression disturbed her. Why did he read with that half-smile? She felt sure that he felt they were "young ladies," "demoiselles," "jeunes filles." She wanted to tell him she was nothing of the kind and take the book from him and show him how to read. His eyes, soft and brown, were the eyes of a child. She noticed that the lower portion of his flat white cheeks looked broader than the upper without giving an effect of squareness of jaw. Then the rhythm took her again and with the second "sur l'eau, si beau," she saw a very blue lake and a little boat with lateen sails, and during the third verse began to forget the lifeless voice. As the murmured refrain came from the girls there was a slight movement in Fraulein's sofa-corner. Miriam did not turn her eyes from Pastor Lahmann's face to look at her, but half expected that at the end of the next verse her low clear devout tones would be heard joining in. Part way through the verse with a startling sweep of draperies against the leather

covering of the sofa, Fraulein stood up and towered extraordinarily tall at Pastor Lahmann's right hand. Her eyes were wide. Miriam thought she had never seen anyone look so pale. She was speaking very quickly in German. Pastor Lahmann rose and faced her. Miriam had just grasped the fact that she was taking the French master to task for reading poetry to his pupils and heard Pastor Lahmann slowly and politely enquire of her whether she or he were conducting the lesson when the two voices broke out together. Fraulein's fiercely voluble and the Herr Pastor's voluble and mocking and polite. The two voices continued as he made his way, bowing gravely, down the far side of the table to the saal doors. Here he turned for a moment and his face shone black and white against the dark panelling. "Na, Kinder," crooned Fraulein gently, when he had disappeared, "a walk--a walk in the beautiful sunshine. Make ready quickly."

"My sainted uncle," laughed Bertha as they trooped down the basement stairs. "Oh--my stars!"

"*Did* you see her eyes?"

"Ja! Wuthend!"

"I wonder the poor little man wasn't burnt up."

"Hurry up, madshuns, we'll have a ripping walk. We'll see if we can go Tiergartenstrasse."

"Does this sort of thing often happen?" asked Miriam, finding herself bending over a boot-box at Gertrude's side.

Gertrude turned and winked at her. "Only sometimes."

"What an awful temper she must have," pursued Miriam.

Gertrude laughed.

## 9

Breakfast the next morning was a gay feast. The mood which had seized the girls at the lavishly decked tea-table awaiting them on their return from their momentous walk the day before, still held them. They all had come in feeling a little apprehensive, and Fraulein behind her tea-urn had met them with the fullest expansion of smiling indulgence Miriam had yet seen. After tea she had suggested an evening's entertainment and had permitted the English girls to act charades.

For Miriam it was an evening of pure delight.  At the end of the first charade, when the girls were standing at a loss in the dimly-lit hall, she made a timid suggestion.  It was enthusiastically welcomed and for the rest of the evening she was allowed to take the lead.  She found herself making up scene after scene surrounded by eager faces.  She wondered whether her raised voice, as she disposed of proffered suggestions--"no, that wouldn't be clear, *this* is the thing we've got to bring out"--could be heard by Fraulein sitting waiting with the Germans under the lowered lights in the saal, and she felt Fraulein's eye on her as she plunged from the hall into the dim schoolroom rapidly arranging effects in the open space in front of the long table which had been turned round and pushed alongside the windows.

Towards the end of the evening, dreaming alone in the schoolroom near the closed door of the little room whence the scenes were lit, she felt herself in a vast space.  The ceilings and walls seemed to disappear.  She wanted a big scene, something quiet and serious--quite different from the fussy little absurdities they had been rushing through all the evening.  A statue . . . one of the Germans.  "You think of something this time," she said, pushing the group of girls out into the hall.

Ulrica.  She must manage to bring in Ulrica without giving her anything to do.  Just to have her to look at.  The height of darkened room above her rose to a sky.  An animated discussion, led by Bertha Martin, was going on in the hall.

They had chosen "beehive."  It would be a catch.  Fraulein was always calling them her Bienenkorb and the girls would guess Bienenkorb and not discover that they were meant to say the English word.

"The old things can't possibly get it.  It'll be a lark, just for the end," said Jimmie.

"No."  Miriam announced radiantly.  "They'd hate a sell.  We'll have Romeo."

"That'll be awfully long.  Four bits altogether, if they don't guess from the syllables," objected Solomon wearily.

Rapidly planning farcical scenes for the syllables she carried her tired troupe to a vague appreciation of the final tableau for Ulrica.  Shrouding the last syllable beyond recognition, she sent a messenger to the audience through the hall door of the saal to beg for Ulrica.

Ulrica came, serenely wondering, her great eyes alight with her evening's enjoyment and was induced by Miriam.

"You've only to stand and look down-nothing else." To mount the schoolroom table in the dimness and standing with her hands on the back of a draped chair to gaze down at Romeo's upturned face.

Bertha Martin's pale profile, with her fair hair drawn back and tied at the nape of her neck and a loose cloak round her shoulders would, it was agreed, make the best presentation of a youth they could contrive, and Miriam arranged her, turning her upturned face so that the audience would catch its clear outline. But at the last minute, urged by Solomon's disapproval of the scene, Bertha withdrew. Miriam put on the cloak, lifted its collar to hide her hair and standing with her back to the audience flung up her hands towards Ulrica as the gas behind the little schoolroom door was turned slowly up. Standing motionless, gazing at the pale oval face bending gravely towards her from the gloom, she felt for a moment the radiance of stars above her and heard the rustle of leaves. Then the guessing voices broke from the saal. "Ach! ach! Wie schon! Romeo! That is beautifoll. Romeo! Who is our Romeo?" and Fraulein's smiling, singing, affectionate voice, "Who is Romeo! The rascal!"

10

Taking the top flight three stairs at a time Miriam reached the garret first and began running about the room at a quick trot with her fists closed, arms doubled and elbows back. The high garret looked wonderfully friendly and warm in the light of her single candle. It seemed full of approving voices. Perhaps one day she would go on the stage. Eve always said so.

People always liked her if she let herself go. She would let herself go more in future at Waldstrasse.

It was so jolly being at Waldstrasse.

"Qu'est-ce que vous avez?" appealed Mademoiselle, laughing at the door with open face. Miriam continued her trot. Mademoiselle put the candle down on the dressing-table and began to run, too, in little quick dancing steps, her wincey skirt bellowing out all round her. Their shadows bobbed and darted, swelling and shrinking on the plaster walls. Soon breathless, Mademoiselle sank down on the side of her bed, panting and volleying raillery and broken tinkles of laughter at Miriam standing goosestepping on the strip of matting with an open. umbrella held high over her head. Recovering breath, she began to lament. . . . Miriam had not during the whole evening of dressing up seen the Martins' summer hats. . . . They were wonderful. Shutting her umbrella Miriam went to her dressing-table drawer. . . . It would be impossible, absolutely impossible . . . to imagine hats more beautiful. . . . Miriam sat on her own bed punctuating through a paper-covered comb. . . . Mademoiselle persisted . . . non, ecoutez--figurez-vous--the hats were of a pale straw . . . the colour of pepper . . . "Bee . . ." responded the comb on a short low wheeze. "And the trimmings--ah, of a charm that no one could describe." . . . "Beem!" squeaked the comb . . . "stalks of barley" . . . "beem-beem" . . . "of a perfect naturalness" . . . "and the flowers, poppies, of a beauty"--"bee-eeem--beeem" . . . "oh, oh, vraiment"--Mademoiselle buried her face in her pillow and put her fingers to her ears.

Miriam began playing very softly "The March of the Men of Harlech," and got to her feet and went marching gently round the room near the walls. Sitting up, Mademoiselle listened. Presently she rounded her eyes and pointed with one finger to the dim roof of the attic.

"Les toiles, d'araignees auront peur!" she whispered.

Miriam ceased playing and her eyes went up to the little window frames high in the wall, farthest away from the island made by their two little beds and the matting and toilet chests and scarcely visible in the flickering candle-light, and came back to Mademoiselle's face.

"Les toiles d'araignees," she breathed, straining her eyes to their utmost size. They gazed at each other. "Les toiles . . ."

Mademoiselle's laughter came first. They sat holding each other's eyes, shaken with laughter, until Mademoiselle said, sighing brokenly, "Et c'est la cloche qui va sonner immediatement." As they undressed, she went on talking--"the night comes the black night . . . we must sleep . . . we must sleep in peace . . . we are safe . . . we are protected . . . nous craignons Dieu, n'est ce pas?" Miriam was shocked to find her at her elbow, in her nightgown, speaking very gravely. She looked for a moment into the serious eyes challenging her own. The mouth was frugally compressed. "Oh yes," said Miriam stiffly.

They blew out the candle when the bell sounded and got into bed. Miriam imagined the Martins' regular features under their barley and poppy trimmed hats.

She knew exactly the kind of English hat it would be.  They were certainly not
pretty hats--she wondered at Mademoiselle's French eyes being so impressed.  She
knew they must be hats with very narrow brims, the trimming coming nearly to
the edge and Solomon's she felt sure inclined to be boat-shaped.  Mademoiselle was
talking about translated English books she had read.  Miriam was glad of her thin
voice piercing the darkness--she did not want to sleep.  She loved the day that had
gone; and the one that was coming.  She saw the room again as it had been when
Mademoiselle had looked up towards the toiles d'araignees.  She had never thought
of there being cobwebs up there.  Now she saw them dangling in corners, high up
near those mysterious windows unnoticed, looking down on her and Mademoiselle
. . . Fraulein Pfaff's cobwebs.  They were hers now, had been hers through cold dark
nights. . . . Mademoiselle was asking her if she knew a most charming English book
. . . "La Premiere Priere de Jessica"?

"Oh yes."

"Oh, the most beautiful book it would be possible to read."  An indrawn breath,
"Le Secret de Lady Audley."

"Yes," responded Miriam sleepily.


11


After the gay breakfast Miriam found herself alone in the schoolroom.  listening inadvertently to a conversation going on apparently in Fraulein Pfaff's room
beyond the little schoolroom.  The voices were low, but she knew neither of them,
nor could she distinguish words.  The sound of the voices, boxed in, filling a little
space shut off from the great empty hall made the house seem very still.  The saal
was empty, the girls were upstairs at their housework.  Miriam restlessly rising
early had done her share before breakfast.  She took Harriett's last letter from her
pocket and fumbled the disarranged leaves for the conclusion.

"We are sending you out two blouses.  Don't you think you're lucky?"  Miriam
glanced out at the young chestnut leaves drooping in tight pleats from black twigs
. . . "real grand proper blouses the first you've ever had, and a skirt to wear them
with . . . won't you be within an inch of your life!  Mother got them at Grigg's--one
is squashed strawberry with a sort of little catherine-wheely design in black going

over it but not too much, awfully smart; and the other is a sort of buffy; one zephyr, the other cotton, and the skirt is a sort of mixey pepper and salt with lumps in the weaving--you know how I mean, something like our prawn dresses only lighter and much more refined. The duffer is going to join the tennis-club--he was at the Pooles' dance. I was simply flabbergasted. He's a duffer."

The little German garden was disappearing from Miriam's eyes. . . . It was cruel, cruel that she was not going to wear her blouses at home, at the tennis-club . . . with Harriett. . . . It was all beginning again, after all--the spring and tennis and presently boating--things were going on . . . the smash had not come . . . why had she not stayed . . . just one more spring? . . . how silly and hurried she had been, and there at home in the garden lilac was quietly coming out and syringa and guelder roses and May and laburnum and . . . everything . . . and she had run away, proud of herself, despising them all, and had turned herself into Miss Henderson, . . . and no one would ever know who she was. . . . Perhaps the blouses would make a difference--it must be extraordinary to have blouses. . . . Slommucky . . . untidy and slommucky Lilla's mother had called them . . . and perhaps they would not fit her. . . .

One of the voices rose to a sawing like the shrill whir of wood being cut by machinery. . . . A derisive laugh broke into the strange sound. It was Fraulein Pfaff's laughter and was followed by her voice thinner and shriller and higher than the other. Miriam listened. What could be going on? . . . both voices were almost screaming . . . together . . . one against the other . . . it was like mad women. . . . A door broke open on a shriek. Miriam bounded to the schoolroom door and opened it in time to see Anna lurch, shouting and screaming, part way down the basement stairs. She turned, leaning with her back against the wall, her eyes half-closed, sawing with fists in the direction of Fraulein, who stood laughing in her doorway. After one glance Miriam recoiled. They had not seen her.

"Ja," screamed Fraulein--"Sie konnen ihre paar Groschen haben!--Ihre paar Groschen! Ihre paar Groschen!" and then the two voices shrieked incoherently together until Fraulein's door slammed to and Anna's voice, shouting and swearing, died away towards the basement.

12

Miriam had crept back to the schoolroom window. She stood shivering, trying to forget the taunting words, and the cruel laughter. "You can have your ha'pence!" Poor Anna. Her poor wages. Her bony face. . .

Gertrude looked in.

"I say, Henderson, come on down and help me pack up lunch. We're all going to Hoddenheim for the day, the whole family, come on."

"For the day?"

"The day, ja. Lily's restless."

Miriam stood looking at her laughing face and listening to her hoarse, whispering voice. Gertrude turned and went downstairs.

Miriam followed her, cold and sick and shivering, and presently glad to be her assistant as she bustled about the empty kitchen,

Upstairs the other girls were getting ready for the outing.

13

Starting out along the dusty field-girt roadway leading from the railway station to the little town of Hoddenheim through the hot sunshine, Miriam was already weary and fearful of the hours that lay ahead. They would bring tests; and opportunities for Fraulein to see all her incapability. Fraulein had thrown her thick gauze veil back over her large hat and was walking with short footsteps, quickly along the centre of the roadway throwing out exclamations of delight, calling to the girls in a singing voice to cast away the winter, to fill their lungs, fill their hearts with spring.

She rallied them to observation.

Miriam could not remember having seen men working in fields. They troubled her. They looked up with strange eyes. She wished they were not there. She wanted the fields to be still--and smaller. Still green fields and orchards . . . woods. . . .

They passed a farmyard and stopped in a cluster at the gate.

There was a moment of relief for her here. She could look easily at the scatter of poultry and the little pigs trotting and grunting about the yard.

She talked to the nearest German girl, of these and of the calves standing in the shelter of a rick, carefully repeating the English names. As her eyes reached the rick she found that she did not know what to say. Was it hay or straw? What was the difference? She dreaded the day more and more.

Fraulein passed on leading the way, down the road hand-in-hand with Emma. The girls straggled after her.

14

Making some remark to Minna, Miriam secured her companionship and dropped a little behind the group. Minna gave her one eager beam from behind her nose, which was shining rosily in the clear air, and they walked silently along side by side bringing up the rear.

Voices and the scrabble of feet along the roadway sounded ahead.

Miriam noticed large rounded puffs of white cloud standing up sharp and still upon the horizon. Cottages began to appear at the roadside.

Standing and moving in the soft air was the strong sour smell of baking schwarz-brot. A big bony-browed woman came from a dark cottage and stood motionless in the low doorway, watching them with kindly body. Miriam glanced at her face--her eyes were small and expressionless, like Anna's . . . evil-looking.

Presently they were in a narrow street. Miriam's footsteps hurried. She almost cried aloud. The fa ades of the dwellings passing slowly on either hand were higher, here and there one rose to a high peak, pierced geometrically with tiny windows. The street widening out ahead showed an open cobbled space and cross-roads. At every angle stood high quiet peaked houses, their faces shining warm cream and milk-white, patterned with windows.

They overtook the others drawn up in the roadway before a long low wooden house. Miriam had time to see little gilded figures standing out in niches in rows all along the fa ade and rows of scrollwork dimly painted, as she stood still a moment with beating heart behind the group. She heard Fraulein talking in English of councillors and centuries and assumed for a moment as Fraulein's eye passed her a look of intelligence; then they had all moved on together deeper into the town.

She clung to Minna, talking at random . . . did she like Hoddenheim . . . and Minna responded to the full, helping her, talking earnestly and emphatically about food and the sunshine, isolating the two of them; and they all reached the cobbled open space and stood still and the peaked houses stood all round them.

15

"You like old-time Germany, Miss Henderson?"

Miriam turned a radiant face to Fraulein Pfaff's table and made some movement with her lips.

"I think you have something of the German in you."

"She has, she has," said Minna from the little arbour where she sat with Millie. "She is not English."

They had eaten their lunch at a little group of arboured tables at the back of an old wooden inn.  Fraulein had talked history to those nearest to her and sat back at last with her gauze veil in place, tall and still in her arbour, sighing happily now and again and making her little sounds of affectionate raillery as the girls finished their coffee and jested and giggled together across their worm-eaten, green-painted tables.

"You have beautiful old towns and villages in England," said Fraulein, yawning slightly.

"Yes--but not anything like this."

"Oh, Gertrude, that isn't true.  We *have.*"

"Then they're hidden from view, my dear Mill, not visible to the naked eye," laughed Gertrude.

"Tell us, my Millie," encouraged Fraulein, "say what you have in mind.  Perhaps Gairtrud does not know the English towns and villages as well as you do."

The German girls attended eagerly.

"I can't tell you the names of the places," said Millie, "but I have seen pictures."

There was a pause.  Gertrude smiled, but made no further response.

"Peectures," murmured Minna.  "Peectures always are beautiful.  All towns are beautiful, perhaps.  Not?"

"There may be bits, perhaps," blurted Miriam, "but not whole towns and nothing anywhere a bit like Hoddenheim, I'm perfectly certain."

"Oh, well, not the *same*," complained Millie, "but just as beautiful--more beautiful."

"Oh-ho, Millississimo."

"Of course there are, Bertha, there must be."

"Well, Millicent," pressed Fraulein, "'more beautiful' and why? Beauty is what you see and is not for everyone the same. It is an affaire de gožt. So you must tell us why to you the old towns of England are more beautiful than the old towns of Germany. It is because you prefair them? They are your towns, it is quite natural you should prefair them."

"It isn't only that, Fraulein."

"Well?"

"Our country is older than Germany, besides--"

"It *isn't*, my blessed child."

"It is, Gertrude--our civilisation."

"Oh, civilisation."

"Englanderin, Englanderin," mocked Bertha.

"Englishwooman, very Englishwooman," echoed Elsa Speier.

"Well, I *am* Englanderin," said Millie, blushing crimson.

"Would you rather the street-boys called Englanderin after you or they didn't?"

"Oh, Jimmie," said Solomon impatiently.

"I wasn't asking you, Solomon."

"What means Solomon, with her 'Oh, Djimmee,' 'oh, Djim *mee'?*"

Solomon stirred heavily and looked up, flushing, her eyes avoiding the German arbours.

"Na, Solemn," laughed Fraulein Pfaff.

"Oh well, of course, Fraulein." Solomon sat in a crimson tide, bridling.

"Solomon likes not Germans."

"Go on, Elsa," rattled Bertha. "Germans are all right, me dear. I think it's rather a lark when they sing out Englanderin. I always want to yell 'Ya!'"

"Likewise 'Boo!' Come on, Mill, we're all waiting."

"Well, you *know* I don't like it, Jimmie."

" *Why?*"

"Because it makes me forget I'm in Germany and only remember I've got to go back."

"My hat, Mill, you're a queer mixture!"

"But, Millie, best child, it's just the very thing that makes you know you're here."

"It doesn't me, Gertrude."

"What is English towns looking like," said Elsa Speier.

No one seemed ready to take up this challenge.

"Like other towns I suppose," laughed Jimmie.

"Our Millie is glad to be in Germany," ruled Fraulein, rising. "She and I agree- -I go most gladly to England.  Gairtrud is neither English nor German.  Perhaps she looks down upon us all."

"Of course I do," roared Gertrude, crossing her knees and tilting her chair. "What do you think?  Was denkt ihr?  I am a barbarian."

"A stranger."

"Still we of the wild are the better men."

"Ah.  We end then with a quotation from our dear Schiller.  Come, children."

"What's that from?" Miriam asked of Gertrude as they wandered up the garden.

"'The Rauber.'  Magnificent thing.  Play.  We saw it last winter."

"I don't believe she really cares for it a bit," was Miriam's mental comment. Her heart was warm towards Millie, looking so outlandish with her English vicarage air in this little German beer-garden, with her strange love of Germany.  Of course there wasn't anything a bit like Germany in England. . . . So silly to make comparisons. "Comparisons are odious."  Perfectly true.

16

They made their way back to the street through a long low roomful of men drinking at little tables.  Heavy clouds of smoke hung and moved in the air and mingled with the steady odour of German food, braten, onion and butter-sodden,

beer and rich sour bread.  A tinkling melody supported by rhythmic time-marking
bass notes that seemed to thump the wooden floor came from a large glass-framed
musical box.  The dark rafters ran low, just above them.  Faces glanced towards
them as they all filed avertedly through the room.  There were two or three guttural
greetings--"N' Morgen, Meine Damen. . . ." A large limber woman met them in the
front room with their bill and stood talking to Fraulein as the girls straggled out
into the sunshine.  She was wearing a neat short-skirted crimson-and-brown check
dress and a large blue apron and her haggard face was lit with radiantly kind strong
dark eyes.  Miriam envied her.  She would like to pour out beer for those simple
men and dispense their food . . . quietly and busily. . . . No need to speak to them, or
be clever.  They would like her care and would understand.  "Meine Damen" hurt
her.  She was not Dame--Was Fraulein? Elsa? Millie was.  Millie would condescend
to these men without feeling uncomfortable.  She could see Millie at village teas. .
. . The girls looked very small as they stood in groups about the roadway. . . . Their
clothes . . . their funny confidence . . . being so sure of themselves . . . what was it .
. . what were they so sure of? There was nothing . . . and she was afraid of them all,
even of Minna and Emma sometimes.

They trailed, Minna once more safely at her side, slowly on through the streets
of the close-built peaked and gabled, carved and cobbled town.  It came nearer to
her than Barnes, nearer even than the old first house she had kissed the morning
they came away--the flower-filled garden, the river, the woods.

They turned aside and up a little mounting street and filed into a churchyard.
Fraulein tried and opened the great carved doorway of the church . . . incense. . . .
They were going into a Roman Catholic church.  How easy it was; just to walk in.
Why had one never done it before? There was one at Roehampton.  But it would
be different in England.

"Pas convenable," she heard Mademoiselle say just behind her, "non, je con-
nais ces gens-la, je vous promets . . . vraiment j'en ai peur. . . ." Elsa responded with
excited enquiries.  They all trooped quietly in and the great doors closed behind
them.

"Vraiment j'ai peur," whispered Mademoiselle.

Miriam saw a point of red light shining like a ruby far ahead in the gloom.  She
went round the church with Fraulein Pfaff and Minna, and was shown stations and

chapels, altars hung with offerings, a dusty tinsel-decked, gaily-painted Madonna, an alcove railed off and fitted with an iron chandelier furnished with spikes--filled half-way up its height by a solid mass of waxen drippings--banners and paintings and artificial flowers, rich dark carvings. She looked at everything and spoke once or twice.

"This is the first time I have seen a Roman Catholic church," she said, "and 'how superstitious' when they came upon crutches and staves hanging behind a reredos--and all the time she breathed the incense and felt the dimness around her and going up and up and brooding, high up.

Presently they were joined by a priest. He took them into a little room, unlocking a heavy door which clanged to after them, opening out behind one of the chapels. One side of the room was lined with an oaken cupboard.

"Je frissonne."

Miriam escaped Mademoiselle's neighbourhood and got into an angle between the frosted window and the plaster wall. The air was still and musty--the floor was of stone, the ceiling low and white. There was nothing in the room but the oaken cupboard. The priest was showing a cross so crusted with jewels that the mounting was invisible. Miriam saw it as he lifted it from its wrappings in the cupboard. It seemed familiar to her. She did not wish to see it more closely, to touch it. She stood as thing after thing was taken from the cupboard, waiting in her corner for the moment when they must leave. Now and again she stepped forward and appeared to look, smiled and murmured. Faint sounds from the town came up now and again.

The minutes were passing; soon they must go. She wanted to stay . . . more than she had ever wanted anything in her life she wanted to stay in this little musty room behind the quiet dim church in this little town.

17

At sunset they stood on a hill outside the town and looked across at it lying up its own hillside, its buildings peaking against the sky. They counted the rich green copper cupolas and sighed and exulted over the whole picture, the coloured sky, the coloured town, the shimmering of the trees.

Making their way along the outskirts of the town towards the station in the fading light they met a little troop of men and women coming quietly along the roadway. They were all dressed in black. They looked at the girls with strange mild eyes and filled Miriam with fear.

Presently the girls crossed a little high bridge over a stream, and from the crest of the bridge beyond a high-walled garden a terraced building came into sight. It was dotted with women dressed in black. One of the figures rose and waved a handkerchief. "Wave, children," said Fraulein's trembling voice, "wave"--and the girls collected in a little group on the crest of the bridge and waved with raised arms.

"Ghastly, isn't it?" said Gertrude, glancing at Miriam as they moved on. Miriam was cold with apprehension. "Are they mad?" she whispered.

## 18

For a week the whole of the housework and cooking was done by the girls under the superintendence of Gertrude, who seemed to be all over the house acting as forewoman to little gangs of workers. Miriam took but a small part in the work--Minna was paying long visits to the aurist every day--but she shared the depleted table and knew that the whole school was taking part in weathering the storm of Fraulein's ill-humour that had broken first upon Anna. She once caught a glimpse of Gertrude flushed and downcast, confronting Fraulein's reproachful voice upon the stairs; and one day in the basement she heard Ulrica tearfully refuse to clean her own boots and saw Fraulein stand before her bowing and smiling, and with the girls gathered round, herself brush and polish the slender boots.

She was glad to get away with Minna.

Her blouses came at the beginning of the week. She carried them upstairs. Her hands took them incredulously from their wrappages. The "squashed strawberry" lay at the top, soft warm clear madder-rose, covered with a black arabesque of tiny leaves and tendrils. It was compactly folded, showing only its turned-down collar, shoulders and breast. She laid it on her bed side by side with its buff companion and shook out the underlying skirt. . . . How sweet of them to send her the things . . . she felt tears in her eyes as she stood at her small looking-glass with the skirt against her body and the blouses held in turn above it . . . they both went perfectly with the light skirt. . . . She unfolded them and shook them out and held them up at arms' length by the shoulder seams. Her heart sank. They were not in the least like anything she had ever worn. They had no shape. They were square and the sleeves were like bags. She turned them about and remembered the shapeliness of the stockinette jerseys smocked and small and clinging that she had worn at school. If these were blouses then she would never be able to wear blouses. . . . "They're so flountery!" she said, frowning at them. She tried on the rose-coloured one. It startled her with its brightness. . . . "It's no good, it's no good," she said, as her hands fumbled for the fastenings. There was a hook at the neck; that was all. Frightful . . . she fastened it, and the collar set in a soft roll but came down in front to the base of her neck. The rest of the blouse stuck out all round her . . . "it's got no cut . . . they couldn't have looked at it." . . . She turned helplessly about, using her hand-glass, frowning and despairing. Presently she saw Harriett's quizzical eyes and laughed woefully, tweaking at the outstanding margin of the material. "It's all very well," she murmured angrily, "but it's all I've *got*." . . . She wished Sarah were there. Sarah would do something, alter it or something. She heard her encouraging voice saying, "You haven't half got it on yet. It'll be all right." She unfastened her black skirt, crammed the flapping margin within its band and put on the beaded black stuff belt.

The blouse bulged back and front shapelessly and seemed to be one with the shapeless sleeves which ended in hard loose bands riding untrimmed about her wrists with the movements of her hands. . . . "It's like a nightdress," she said wrathfully and dragged the fulnesses down all round under her skirt. It looked better so in front; but as she turned with raised hand-glass it came riding up at the side and back with the movement of her arm.

19

Minna was calling to her from the stairs. She went on to the landing to answer her and found her on the top flight dressed to go out.

"Ach!" she whispered as Miriam drew back. "Jetzt mag' ich sie leiden. *Now* I like you."

She ran back to her room. There was no time to change. She fixed a brooch in the collar to make it come a little higher at the join.

Going downstairs she saw Pastor Lahmann hanging up his hat in the hall. His childish eyes came up as her step sounded on the lower flight.

Miriam was amazed to see him standing there as though nothing had happened. She did not know that she was smiling at him until his face lit up with an answering smile.

"Bonjour, mademoiselle."

Miriam did not answer and he disappeared into the saal.

She went on downstairs listening to his voice, repeating his words over and over in her mind.

Jimmie was sweeping the basement floor with a duster tied round her hair.

"Hullo, Mother Bunch," she laughed.

"It *is* weird, isn't it? Not a bit the kind I meant to have."

"The blouse is all right, my dear, but it's all round your ears and you've got all the fulness in the wrong place. There. . . . Bless the woman, you've got no drawstring! And you must pin it at the back! And haven't you got a proper leather belt?"

20

Minna and Miriam ambled gently along together. Miriam had discarded her little fur pelerine and her double-breasted jacket bulged loosely over the thin fabric of her blouse. She breathed in the leaf-scented air and felt it playing over her breast and neck. She drew deep breaths as they went slowly along under the Waldstrasse lime-trees and looked up again and again at the leaves brilliant opaque green against white plaster with sharp black shadows behind them, or brilliant transparent green on the hard blue sky. She felt that the scent of them must be visible. Every breath she drew was like a long yawning sigh. She felt the easy expansion of her body under her heavy jacket. . . . "Perhaps I won't have any more fitted bodices," she mused and was back for a moment in the stale little sitting-room of the Barnes dressmaker. She remembered deeply breathing in the odour of fabrics and dust and dankness and cracking her newly fitted lining at the pinholes and saying, "It is too tight there"--crack-crack. "I can't go like that" . . .

"But you never want to go like that, my dear child," old Miss Ottridge had laughed, readjusting the pins; "just breathe in your ordinary way--there, see? That's right."

Perhaps Lilla's mother was right about blouses . . . perhaps they were "slom-mucky." She remembered phrases she had heard about people's figures . . . "falling abroad" . . . "the middle-aged sprawl" . . . that would come early to her as she was so old and worried . . . perhaps that was why one had to wear boned bodices . . . and never breathe in gulps of air like this? . . . It was as if all the worry were being taken out of her temples. She felt her eyes grow strong and clear; a coolness flowed through her--obstructed only where she felt the heavy pad of hair pinned to the back of her head, the line of her hat, the hot line of compression round her waist and the confinement of her inflexible boots.

They were approaching the Georgstrasse with its long-vistaed width and its shops and cafes and pedestrians. An officer in pale blue Prussian uniform passed by flashing a single hard preoccupied glance at each of them in turn. His eyes seemed to Miriam like opaque blue glass. She could not remember such eyes in England. They began to walk more quickly. Miriam listened abstractedly to Minna's antici-pations of three days at a friend's house when she would visit her parents at the end of the week. Minna's parents, her far-away home on the outskirts of a little town, its garden, their little carriage, the spring, the beautiful country seemed unreal and her efforts to respond and be interested felt like a sort of treachery to her present bliss. . . . Everybody, even docile Minna, always seemed to want to talk about some-thing else. . . .

Suddenly she was aware that Minna was asking her whether, if it was decided that she should leave school at the end of the term, she, Miriam, would come and live with her.

Miriam beamed incredulously. Minna, crimson-faced, with her eyes on the pavement and hurrying along explained that she was alone at home, that she had never made friends--her mother always wanted her to make friends--but she could not--that her parents would be so delighted--that she, she wanted Miriam, "You, you are so different, so--reasonable--I could live with you."

Minna's garden, her secure country house, her rich parents, no worries, nothing particular to do, seemed for a moment to Miriam the solution and continuation of all the gay day. There would be the rest of the term--increasing spring and summer--Fraulein divested of all mystery and fear and then freedom--with Minna.

She glanced at Minna--the cheerful pink face and the pink bulb of nose came round to her and in an excited undertone she murmured something about the apotheker.

"I should love to come--simply love it," said Miriam enthusiastically, feeling that she would not entirely give up the idea yet. She would not shut off the offered refuge. It would be a plan to have in reserve. She had been daunted as Minna murmured by a picture of Minna and herself in that remote garden--she receiving confidences about the apotheker--no one else there--the Waldstrasse household blotted out--herself and Minna finding pretexts day after day to visit the chemist's in the little town.

21

Miriam almost ran home from seeing Minna into the three o'clock train . . . dear beautiful, beautiful Hanover . . . the sunlight blazed from the rain-sprinkled streets. Everything shone. Bright confident shops, happy German cafes moved quickly by as she fled along. Sympathetic eyes answered hers. She almost laughed once or twice when she met an eye and thought how funny she must look "tearing along" with her long, thick, black jacket bumping against her. . . . She would leave it off to-morrow and go out in a blouse and her long black lace scarf. She imagined Harriett at her side--Harriett's long scarf and longed to do the "crab walk" for a moment or the halfpenny dip, hippety-hop. She did them in her mind.

She heard the sound of her boot soles tapping the shining pavement as she hurried along . . . she would write a short note to her mother "a girl about my own age with very wealthy parents who wants a companion" and enclose a note for Eve or Harriett . . . Eve, "Imagine me in Pomerania, my dear" . . . and tell her about the coffee parties and the skating and the sleighing and Minna's German Christmasses. . . .

She saw Minna's departing face leaning from the carriage window, its new gay boldness: "I shall no more when we are at home call you Miss Henderson."

When she got back to Waldstrasse she found Anna's successor newly arrived cleaning the neglected front doorstep.  Her lean yellow face looked a vacant response to Miriam's enquiry for Fraulein Pfaff.

"Ist Fraulein zu Hause," she repeated.  The girl shook her head vaguely.

How quiet the house seemed.  The girls, after a morning spent in turning out the kitchen for the reception of the new *magd* were out for a long ramble, including *Schocolade mit Schlagsahne* until tea-time.

The empty house spread round her and towered above her as she took off her things in the basement and the schoolroom yawned bright and empty as she reached the upper hall.  She hesitated by the door.  There was no sound anywhere. . . . She would play . . . on the saal piano.

"I'm not a Lehrerin--I'm not--I'm--not," she hummed as she collected her music . . . she would bring her songs too. . . . "I'm going to Pom--pom--pom--Pom-erain--eeya."

22

"Pom--erain--eeya," she hummed, swinging herself round the great door into the saal.  Pastor Lahmann was standing near one of the windows.  The rush of her entry carried her to the middle of the room and he met her there smiling quietly.  She stared easily and comfortably up into his great mild eyes, went into them as they remained quietly and gently there, receiving her.  Presently he said in a soft low tone, "You are vairy happy, mademoiselle."

Miriam moved her eyes from his face and gazed out of the window into the little sunlit summer-house.  The sense of the outline of his shoulders and his comforting black mannishness so near to her brought her almost to tears.  Fiercely she fixed the sunlit summer-house, "Oh, I'm *not,*" she said.

"Not?  Is it possible?"

"I think life is perfectly appalling."

She moved awkwardly to a little chiffonier and put down her music on its marble top.

He came safely following her and stood near again.

"You do not like the life of the school?"

"Oh, I don't know."

"You are from the country, mademoiselle."

Miriam fumbled with her music. . . . Was she?

"One sees that at once. You come from the land."

Miriam glanced at his solid white profile as he stood with hands clasped, near her music, on the chiffonier. She noticed again that strange flatness of the lower part of the face.

"I, too, am from the land. I grew up on a farm. I love the land and think to return to it--to have my little strip when I am free--when my boys have done their schooling. I shall go back."

He turned towards her and Miriam smiled into the soft brown eyes and tried to think of something to say.

"My grandfather was a gentleman-farmer."

"Ah--that does not surprise me--but what a very English expression!"

"Is it?"

"Well, it sounds so to us. We Swiss are very democratic."

"I think I'm a radical."

Pastor Lahmann lifted his chin and laughed softly.

"You are a vairy ambitious young lady."

"Yes."

Pastor Lahmann laughed again.

"I, too, am ambitious. I have a good Swiss ambition."

Miriam smiled into the mild face.

"You have a beautiful English provairb which expresses my ambition."

Miriam looked, eagerly listening, into the brown eyes that came round to meet hers, smiling:

"A little land, well-tilled, A little wife, well-willed, Are great riches."

Miriam seemed to gaze long at a pallid, rounded man with smiling eyes. She saw a garden and fields, a firelit interior, a little woman smiling and busy and agreeable moving quickly about. . . . and Pastor Lahmann--presiding. It filled her with fury to be regarded as one of a world of little tame things to be summoned by little men to be well-willed wives. She must make him see that she did not even recognise such a thing as "a well-willed wife." She felt her gaze growing fixed and moved to withdraw it and herself.

"Why do you wear glasses, mademoiselle?"

The voice was full of sympathetic wistfulness.

"I have a severe myopic astigmatism," she announced, gathering up her music and feeling the words as little hammers on the newly seen, pallid, rounded face.

"Dear me . . . I wonder whether the glasses are really necessary. . . . May I look at them? . . . I know something of eye-work."

Miriam detached her tightly fitting pince-nez and having given them up stood with her music in hand anxiously watching.  Half her vision gone with her glasses, she saw only a dim black-coated knowledge, near at hand, going perhaps to help her.

"You wear them always--for how long?"

"Poor child, poor child, and you must have passed through all your schooling with those lame, lame eyes . . . let me see the eyes . . . turn a little to the light . . . so." Standing near and large he scrutinised her vague gaze.

"And sensitive to light, too.  You were vairy, vairy blonde, even more blonde than you are now, as a child, mademoiselle?"

"Na guten Tag, Herr Pastor."

Fraulein Pfaff's smiling voice sounded from the little door.

Pastor Lahmann stepped back.

Miriam was pleased at the thought of being grouped with him in the eyes of Fraulein Pfaff.  As she took her glasses from his outstretched hand she felt that Fraulein would recognise that they had established a kind of friendliness.  She halted for a moment at the door, adjusting her glasses, amiably uncertain, feeling for something to say.

Pastor Lahmann was standing in the middle of the room examining his nails. Fraulein, at the window, was twitching a curtain into place.  She turned and drove Miriam from the room with speechless waiting eyes.

The sunlight was streaming across the hall.  It seemed gay and home-like.  Pastor Lahmann had made her forget she was a governess.  He had treated her as a girl. Fraulein's eyes had spoiled it.  Fraulein was angry about it for some extraordinary reason.

# CHAPTER VII

"Don't let her *do* it, Miss Henderson."

Fraulein Pfaff's words broke the silence accompanying the servant's progress from Gertrude whose soup-plate she had first seized, to Miriam more than half-way down the table.

Startled into observation Miriam saw the soup-spoon of her neighbour whisked, dripping, from its plate to the uppermost of Marie's pile and Emma shrinking back with a horrified face against Jimmie who was leaning forward entranced with watching. . . . The whole table was watching. Marie, having secured Emma's plate to the base of her pile clutched Miriam's spoon. Miriam moved sideways as the spoon swept up, saw the desperate hard, lean face bend towards her for a moment as her plate was seized, heard an exclamation of annoyance from Fraulein and little sounds from all round the table. Marie had passed on to Clara. Clara received her with plate and spoon held firmly together and motioned her before she would relinquish them, to place her load upon the shelf of the lift.

Miriam felt she was in disgrace with the whole table. . . . She sat, flaring, rapidly framing phrase after phrase for the lips of her judges . . . "slow and awkward" . . . "never has her wits about her". . . .

"Don't let her do it, Miss Henderson. . . ." Why should Fraulein fix upon *her* to teach her common servants? Struggling through her resentment was pride in the fact that she did not know how to handle soup-plates. Presently she sat refusing absolutely to accept the judgment silently assailing her on all hands.

"You are not very domesticated, Miss Henderson."

"No," responded Miriam quietly, in joy and fear.

Fraulein gave a short laugh.

Goaded, Miriam plunged forward.

"We were never even allowed in the kitchen at home."

"I see. You and your sisters were brought up like Countesses, wie Grafinnen," observed Fraulein Pfaff drily.

Miriam's whole body was on fire . . . "and your sisters and your sisters," echoed through and through her. Holding back her tears she looked full at Fraulein and met the brown eyes. She met them until they turned away and Fraulein broke into smiling generalities. Conversation was released all round the table. Emphatic undertones reached her from the English side. "Fool" . . . "simply idiotic."

"I've done it now," mused Miriam calmly, on the declining tide of her wrath.

Pretending to be occupied with those about her she sat examining the look Fraulein had given her . . . she hates me. . . . Perhaps she did from the first. . . . She did from the first. . . . I shall have to go . . . and suddenly, lately, she has grown worse. . . .

## CHAPTER VIII

### 1

Walking along a narrow muddy causeway by a little river overhung with willows, girls ahead of her in single file and girls in single file behind, Miriam drearily recognised that it was June. The month of roses, she thought, and looked out across the flat green fields. It was not easy to walk along the slippery pathway. On one side was the little grey river, on the other long wet grass repelling and depressing. Not far ahead was the roadway which led, she supposed to the farm where they were to drink new milk. She would have to walk with someone when they came to the road, and talk. She wondered whether this early morning walk would come, now, every day. Her heart sank at the thought. It had been too hot during the last few days for any going out at midday, and she had hoped that the strolling in the garden, sitting about under the chestnut tree and in the little wooden garden room off the saal had taken the place of walks for the summer.

She had got up reluctantly, at the surprise of the very early gonging. Mademoiselle had guessed it would he a "milk-walk." Pausing in the bright light of the top landing as Mademoiselle ran downstairs she had seen through the landing window the deep peak of a distant gable casting an unfamiliar shadow--a shadow sloping the wrong way, a morning shadow. She remembered the first time, the only time, she had noticed such a shadow--getting up very early one morning while Harriett and all the household were still asleep--and how she had stopped dressing and gazed at it as it stood there cool and quiet and alone across the mellow face of a neighbouring stone porch--had suddenly been glad that she was alone and had wondered why that shadowed porch-peak was more beautiful than all the summer things she knew and felt at that moment that nothing could touch or trouble her again.

She could not find anything of that feeling in the early day outside Hanover. She was hemmed in, and the fields were so sad she could not bear to look at them. The sun had disappeared since they came out. The sky was grey and low and it seemed warmer already than it had been in the midday sun during the last few days. One of the girls on ahead hummed the refrain of a student-song:--

"In der Ecke steht er Seinen Schnurbart dreht er Siehst du wohl, da steht er schon Der versoff'ne Schwiegersohn."

Miriam felt very near the end of endurance.

Elsa Speier who was just behind her, became her inevitable companion when they reached the roadway. A farmhouse appeared about a quarter of a mile away.

Miriam's sense of her duties closed in on her. Trying not to see Elsa's elaborate clothes and the profile in which she could find no meaning, no hope, no rest, she spoke to her.

"Do you like milk, Elsa?" she said cheerfully.

Elsa began swinging her lace-covered parasol.

"If I like milk?" she repeated presently, and flashed mocking eyes in Miriam's direction.

Despair touched Miriam's heart.

"Some people don't," she said.

Elsa hummed and swung her parasol.

"Why should I like milk?" she stated.

The muddy farmyard, lying back from the roadway and below it, was steamy and choking with odours. Miriam who had imagined a cool dairy and cold milk frothing in pans, felt a loathing as warmth came to her fingers from the glass she held. Most of the girls were busily sipping. She raised her glass once towards her lips, snuffed a warm reek, and turned away towards the edge of the group, to pour out the contents of her glass, unseen, upon the filth-sodden earth.

2

Passing languidly up through the house after breakfast, unable to decide to spend her Saturday morning as usual at a piano in one of the bedrooms, Miriam went, wondering in response to a quiet call from Fraulein Pfaff into the large room shared by the Bergmanns and Ulrica Hesse. Explaining that Clara was now to take possession of the half of Elsa Speier's room that had been left empty by Minna--"poor Minna now with her good parents seeking health in the Swiss mountains, schooldays at an end, at an end, at an end," she repeated mournfully, Fraulein explained that Clara's third of the large room would now be Miriam's.

Miriam stood incredulous at her side as she indicated a large empty chest of drawers, a white covered bed in a deep corner away from the window, a small drawer in the dressing-table and five pegs in a large French wardrobe. Emma was going very gravely about the room collecting her work-basket and things for *raccommodage.* She flung one ecstatic glance at Miriam as she went away with these.

"I shall hold you responsible here amongst these dear children, Miss Henderson," fluted Fraulein, quietly gathering up a few last things of Minna's collected on the bed, "our dear Ulrica and our little Emma," she smiled, passing out, leaving Miriam standing in the wonderful room.

"My goodney," she breathed, gathering gently clenched fists close to her person. She stood for a few moments; she felt like a visitor . . . embroidered toilet covers, polished furniture, gold and cream crockery, lace curtains, white beds, the large screen cutting off her third of the room . . . then she rushed headlong upstairs, a member of the downstairs landing, to collect her belongings.

On the landing just outside the door of the garret bedroom stood a huge wicker travelling basket; a clumsy umbrella with a large knobby handle, like a man's umbrella, lay on the top of it partly covering a large pair of goloshes.

She was tired and very warm by the time everything was arranged in her new quarters.

Taking a last look round she caught the eye of Eve's photograph gazing steadily at her from the chest of drawers. . . . It would be quite easy now that this had happened to write and tell them that the Pomerania plan had come to nothing.

Evidently Fraulein approved of her, after all.

3

In the schoolroom she found the *raccommodage* party gathered round the table.  At its head sat Mademoiselle, her arms flung out upon the table and her face buried against them.

"Cheer up, Mademoiselle," said Jimmie as Miriam took an empty chair between Gertrude and the Martins.

Timidly meeting Gertrude's eye Miriam received her half-smile, watched her eyebrows flicker faintly up and the little despairing shrug she gave as she went on with her mending.

"Ah, mamma *zell*chen c'est pas mal, ne soyez triste, mein Gott mammazellchen es ist aber nichts!" chided Emma consolingly from her place near the window.

"Oh! je ne veux pas, je ne veux pas," sobbed Mademoiselle.

No one spoke; Mademoiselle lay snuffling and shuddering.  Solomon's scissors fell on to the floor.  "Mais pour *quoi* pas, Mademoiselle?" she interrogated as she recovered them.

"Pourquoi, pourquoi!" choked Mademoiselle.  Her suffused little face came up for a moment towards Solomon.  She met Miriam's gaze as if she did not see her. "Vous me demandez pourquoi je ne veux pas partager ma chambre avec une femine mariee?"  Her head sank again and her little grey form jerked sharply as she sobbed.

"Probably a widder, Mademoiselle," ventured Bertha Martin, "oon voove."

" *Verve,* Bertha," came Millie's correcting voice and Miriam's interest changed to excited thoughts of Fraulein--not hating her, and choosing Mademoiselle to sleep with the servant, a new servant--the things on the landing--Mademoiselle refusing to share a room with a married woman . . . she felt about round this idea as Millie's prim, clear voice went on . . . her eyes clutched at Mademoiselle, begging to understand . . . she gazed at the little down-flung head, fine little tendrils frilling along the edge of her hair, her little hard grey shape, all miserable and ashamed.  It was dreadful.  Miriam felt she could not bear it.  She turned away.  It was a strange new thought that anyone should object to being with a married woman . . . would she object? or Harriett?  Not unless it were suggested to them.

Was there some special refinement in this French girl that none of them understood?  Why should it be refined to object to share a room with a married woman? A cold shadow closed in on Miriam's mind.

"I don't care," said Millie almost quickly, with a crimson face.  "It's a special occasion. I think Mademoiselle ought to complain. If I were in her place I should write home. It's not right. Fraulein has no right to make her sleep with a servant."

"Why can't the servant sleep in one of the back attics?" asked Solomon.

"Not furnished, my sweetheart," said Gertrude, "and you know Kinder you're all running on very fast about servants--the good Frau is our housekeeper."

"Will she have meals with us?"

"Gewiss Jimmie, meals."

"Mon Dieu, vous etes terribles, toutes!" came Mademoiselle's voice. It seemed to bite into the table. "Oh, eest grossiere!" She gathered herself up and escaped into the little schoolroom.

"Armes, armes, Momzell," wailed Ulrica gently gazing out of the window.

"Som one should go, go you, Henchen," urged Emma.

"Don't, for goodness' sake, Hendy," begged Jimmie, "not you, she's wild about you going downstairs," she whispered.

Miriam struggled with her gratification. "Oh go, som one; go you, Clara!"

"Better leave her alone," ruled Gertrude.

"We miss old Minna, don't we?" concluded Bertha.

4

The heat grew intense.

The air was more and more oppressive as the day went on.

Clara fainted suddenly just after dinner, and Fraulein, holding a little discourse on clothing and an enquiry into wardrobes, gave a general permission for the reduction of garments to the minimum and sent everyone to rest uncorseted until tea-time, promising a walk to the woods in the cool of the evening. There was a sense of adventure in the house. It was as if it were being besieged. It gave Miriam confidence to approach Fraulein for permission to rearrange her trunk in the basement. She let Fraulein understand that her removal was not complete, that there were things to do before she could be properly settled in her new room.

"Certainly, Miss Henderson, you are quite free," said Fraulein instantly as the girls trooped upstairs.

Miriam knew she wanted to avoid an afternoon shut up with Emma and Ulrica and she did not in the least want to lie down. It seemed to her a very extraordinary thing to do. It surprised and disturbed her. It suggested illness and weakness. She could not remember having lain down in the daytime. There had been that fortnight in the old room at home with Harriett . . . chicken-pox and new books coming and games, and Sarah reading the Song of Hiawatha and their being allowed to choose their pudding. She could not remember feeling ill. Had she ever felt ill? . . . Colds and bilious attacks. . . .

She remembered with triumph a group of days of pain two years ago. She had forgotten. . . . Bewilderment and pain . . . her mother's constant presence . . . everything, the light everywhere, the leaves standing out along the tops of hedgerows as she drove with her mother, telling her of pain and she alone in the midst of it . . . for always . . . pride, long moments of deep pride. . . . Eve and Sarah congratulating her, Eve stupid and laughing . . . the new bearing of the servants . . . Lily Belton's horrible talks fading away to nothing.

Fraulein had left her and gone to her room. Every door and window on the ground floor stood wide excepting that leading to Fraulein's little double rooms. She wondered what the rooms were like and felt sorry for Fraulein, tall and gaunt, moving about in them alone, alone with her own dark eyes, curtains hanging motionless at the windows . . . was it really bad to tight-lace? The English girls, except Millie and Solomon all had small waists. She wished she knew. She placed her large hands round her waist. Drawing in her breath she could almost make them meet. It was easier to play tennis with stays . . . how dusty the garden looked, baked. She wanted to go out with two heavy watering-cans, to feel them pulling her arms from their sockets, dragging her shoulders down, throwing out her chest, to spray canful after canful through a great wide rose, sprinkling her ankles sometimes, and to grow so warm that she would not feel the heat. Bella Lyndon had never worn stays; playing rounders so splendidly, lying on the grass between the games with her arms under her head . . . simply disgusting, someone had said . . . who . . . a disgusted face . . . nearly all the girls detested Bella.

Going through the hall on her way down to the basement she heard the English voices sounding quietly out into the afternoon from the rooms above. Flat and tranquil they sounded, Bertha and Jimmie she heard, Gertrude's undertones, quiet words from Millie.  She felt she would like a corner in the English room for the afternoon, a book and an occasional remark--"Mr. Barnes of New York"--she would not be able to read her three yellow books in the German bedroom.  She felt at the moment glad to be robbed of them.  It would be much better, of course.  There was no sound from the German rooms.  She pictured sleeping faces.  It was cooler in the basement--but even there the air seemed stiff and dusty with the heat.

Why did the hanging garments remind her of All Saints' Church and Mr. Brough? . . . she must tell Harriett that in her letter . . . that day they suddenly decided to help in the church decorations . . . she remembered the smell of the soot on the holly as they had cut and hacked at it in the cold garden, and Harriett overturning the heavy wheelbarrow on the way to church, and how they had not laughed because they both felt solemn, and then there had just been the three Anwyl girls and Mrs. Anwyl and Mrs. Scarr and Mr. Brough in the church-room all being silly about Birdy Anwyl roasting chestnuts, and how silly and affected they were when a piece of holly stuck in her skirt.

5

Coming up the basement stairs in response to the tea-gong, Miriam thought there were visitors in the hall and hesitated; then there was Pastor Lahmann's profile disappearing towards the door and Fraulein patting and dismissing two of his boys.  His face looked white and clear and firm and undisturbed, Miriam wanted to arrest him and ask him something--what he thought of the weather--he looked so different from her memory of him in the saal two Saturdays ago--two weeks--four classes she must have missed.  Why?  Why was she missing Pastor Lahmann's classes?  How had it happened?  Perhaps she would see him in class again.  Perhaps next week. . . .

The other visitors proved to be the Bergmanns in new dresses.  Miriam gazed at Clara as she went down the schoolroom to her corner of the table.  She looked like . . . a hostess.  It seemed absurd to see her sit down to tea as a school-girl.  The dress was a fine black muslin stamped all over with tiny fish-shaped patches of mauve.  It was cut to the base of the neck and came to a point in front where the soft white ruching was fastened with a large cameo brooch.  Clara's pallid worried face had grown more placid during the hot inactive days, and to-day her hard mouth looked patient and determined and responsible. She seemed quite independent of her sur-roundings. Miriam found herself again and again consulting her calm face. Her presence haunted Miriam throughout tea-time. Emma was sweet, pink and bright after her rest in a bright light brown muslin dress dotted with white spots. . . .

Funny German dresses, thought Miriam, funny . . . and old. Her mind hovered and wondered over these German dresses--did she like them or not--something about them--she glanced at Elsa, sitting opposite in the dull faint electric blue with black lace sleeves she had worn since the warm weather set in. Even Ulrica, thin and straight now . . . like a pole . . . in a tight flat dress of saffron muslin sprigged with brown leaves, seemed to be included in something that made all these German dresses utterly different from anything the English girls could have worn. What was it? It was crowned by the Bergmanns' dresses. It had begun in a summer dress of Minna's, black with a tiny sky-blue spot and a heavy ruche round the hem. She thought she liked it. It seemed to set the full tide of summer round the table more than the things of the English girls--and yet the dresses were ugly--and the English girls' dresses were not that . . . they were nothing . . . plain cottons and zephyrs with lace tuckers--no ruches. It was something somehow in the ruches--the ruches and the little peaks of neck.

A faint scent of camphor came from the Martins across the way, sitting in their cool creased black-and-white check cotton dresses. They still kept to their hard white collars and cuffs. As tea went on Miriam found her eyes drawn back and back again to these newly unpacked camphor-scented dresses . . . and when conversa-tion broke after moments of stillness . . . shadowy foliage . . . the still hot garden . . . the sunbaked wooden room beyond the sunny saal, the light pouring through three rooms and bright along the table . . . it was to the Martins' check dresses that she glanced.

It was intensely hot, but the strain had gone out of the day; the feeling of just bearing up against the heat and getting through the day had gone; they all sat round . . . which was which? . . . Miriam met eye after eye--how beautiful they all were looking out from faces and meeting hers--and her eyes came back unembarrassed to her cup, her solid butterbrot and the sunlit angle of the garden wall and the bit of tree just over Fraulein Pfaff's shoulder. She tried to meet Mademoiselle's eyes, she felt sure their eyes could meet. She wondered intensely what was in Elsa's mind behind her faint hard blue dress. She wanted to hear Mademoiselle's voice; Mademoiselle was almost invisible in her corner near the door, the new housekeeper was sitting at her side very upright and close to the table. Once or twice she felt Fraulein's look; she sustained it, and glowed happily under it without meeting it; she referred back contentedly to it after hearing herself laugh out once just as she would do at home; once or twice she forgot for a moment where she was. The way the light shone on the housekeeper's hair, bright brown and plastered flatly down on either side of her bright white-and-crimson face, and the curves of her chocolate and white striped cotton bodice, reminded her sharply of something she had seen once, something that had charmed her . . . it was in the hair against the hard white of the forehead and the flat broad cheeks with the hard, clear crimson colouring nearly covering them . . . something in the way she sat, standing out against the others. . . . Judy on her left hand with almost the same colouring looked small and gentle and refined.

6

Tea was over. Fraulein decided against a walk and they all trooped into the saal. No programme was suggested; they all sat about unoccupied. There was no centre; Fraulein Pfaff was one of them. The little group near her in the shady half of the sunlit summer-house was as quietly easy as those who sat far back in the saal. Miriam had got into a low chair near the saal doors whence she could see across the room through the summer-house window through the gap between the houses across the way to the far-off afternoon country. Its colours gleamed, a soft confusion of tones, under the heat-haze. For a while she sat with her eyes on Fraulein's thin profile, clean and cool and dry in the intense heat . . . "she must be looking out towards the lime-trees." . . . Ulrica sat drooped on a low chair near her knees . . . "sweet beautiful head" . . . the weight of her soft curved mouth seemed too much for the delicate angles of her face and it drooped faintly, breaking their sharp lines. Miriam wished all the world could see her. . . . Presently Ulrica raised her head, as Elsa and Clara broke into words and laughter near her, and her drooping lips flattened gently back into their place in the curve of her face. She gazed out through the doorway of the summer-house with her great despairing eyes . . . the house-keeper was rather like a Dutch doll . . . but that was not it.

7

The sun had set.  Miriam had found a little thin volume of German poetry in her pocket.  She sat fumbling the leaves.  She felt the touch of her limp straight-ening hair upon her forehead.  It did not matter.  Twilight would soon come, and bed-time.  But it must have been beginning to get like that at tea-time.  Perhaps the weather would get even hotter.  She must do something about her hair . . . if only she could wear it turned straight back.

There was a stirring in the room; beautiful forms rose and stood and spoke and moved about.  Someone went to the door.  It opened gently with a peaceful sound on to the quiet hall and footsteps ran upstairs.  Two figures going out from the saal passed in front of the two still sitting quietly grouped in the light of the summer-house.  They were challenged as they passed and turned soft profiles and stood talk-ing.  Behind the voices,--flutings, single notes, broken phrases, long undisturbed warblings came from the garden.

Clara was at the piano.  Tall behind her stood Millie's gracious shapeless baby-form.

As Millie's voice climbing carefully up and down the even stages of Solveig's song reached the second verse, Miriam tried to separate the music from the words.  The words were wrong.  She half saw a fair woman with a great crown of plaited hair and very broad shoulders singing the song in the Hanover concert-room in Norwegian.  She remembered the moment of taking her eyes away from the singer and the platform, and feeling the crowded room and the airlessness, and then the song going steadily on from note to note as she listened . . . no trills and no tune . . . saying something.  It stood in the air.  All the audience were saying it.  And then the fair-haired woman had sung the second verse as though it was something about herself--tragically . . . tragic muse. . . . It was not her song, standing there in the vel-vet dress. . . . She stopped it from going on.  There was nothing but the movement of the lace round her shoulders and chest, her expanded neck, quivering, and the pressure in her voice. . . . And then there had been Herr Bossenberger, hammering

and shouting it out in the saal with Millie, and everything in the schoolroom, even
the dust on the paper-rack, standing out clearer and clearer as he bellowed slowly
along. And then she had got to know that everybody knew about it; it was a famous
song. There were people singing it everywhere in German and French and English-
-a girl singing about her lover. . . . It was not that; even if people sang it like that, if
a real girl had ever sung something like that, that was not what she meant . . . "the
winter may pass" . . . yes, that was all right--and mountains with green slopes and
narrow torrents--and a voice going strongly out and ceasing, and all the sky filled
with the sound--and the song going on, walking along, thinking to itself. . . . She
looked about as Millie's voice ceased trembling on the last high note. She hoped
no one would hum the refrain. There was no one there who knew anything about
it. . . . Judy? Judy knew, perhaps. Judy would never hum or sing anything. If she
did, it would be terrible. She knew so much. Perhaps Judy knew everything. She
was sitting on the low sill of the window behind the piano sewing steel beads on
to a shot silk waistband held very close to her eyes. Minna could. Minna might be
sitting in her plaid dress on the window-seat with her embroidery, her smooth hair
polished with bay-rum humming Solveig's song.

The housekeeper brought in the milk and rolls and went away downstairs
again. The cold milk was very refreshing but the room grew stifling as they all
sat round near the little centre table with the French window nearly closed, shutting off the summer-house and garden. Everybody in turn seemed to be saying "Ik
kenne meine Tasse sie ist svatz." Bertha had begun it, holding up her white glass of
milk as she took it from the tray and exactly imitating the housekeeper's voice.

"Platt Deutsch spricht-sie, ja?" Clara had said. It seemed as if there were no
more to be said about the housekeeper. At prayers when they were all saying "Vater
unser," she heard Jimmie murmur, "Ik kenne meine Tasse."

8

Fraulein Pfaff came upstairs behind the girls and ordered silence as they went
to their rooms. "Hear, all, children," she said in German in the quiet clear even tone
with which she had just read prayers, "no one to speak to her neighbour, no one
to whisper or bustle, nor to-night to brush her hair, but each to compose her mind

and go quietly to her rest. Thus acting the so great heat shall injure none of us and peaceful sleep will come. Do you hear, children?"

Answering voices came from the bedrooms. She entered each room, shifting screens, opening each window for a few moments, leaving each door wide.

"Each her little corner," she said in Miriam's room, "fresh water set for the morning. The heavens are all round us, my little ones; have no fear."

Gently sighing and moaning Ulrica moved about in her corner. Emma dropped a slipper and muttered consolingly. Thankfully Miriam listened to Fraulein's short, deprecating footsteps pacing up and down the landing. She was safe from the dreadful challenge of conversation with her pupils. She felt hemmed in in the stifling room with the landing full of girls all round her. She wanted to push away her screen, push up the hot white ceiling. She wished she could be safely upstairs with Mademoiselle and the height of the candle-lit garret above her head. It could not possibly be hotter up there than in this stifling room with its draperies and furniture and gas.

Fraulein came in very soon and turned out the light with a formal good-night greeting. For a while after all the lights were out, she continued pacing up and down.

Across the landing someone began to sneeze rapidly sneeze after sneeze. "Ach, die Millie!" muttered Emma sleepily. For several minutes the sneezing went on. Sighs and impatient movements sounded here and there. "Ruhig, Kinder, ruhig. Millie shall soon sleep peacefully as all."

9

Miriam could not remember hearing Fraulein Pfaff go away when she woke in the darkness feeling unendurably oppressed. She flung her sheet aside and turned her pillow over and pushed her frilled sleeves to her elbows. How energetic I am, she thought and lay tranquil. There was not a sound. "I shall never be able to sleep down here, it's too awful," she murmured, and puffed and shifted her head on the pillow.

The Win-ter may--pass. . . . The win-ter . . . may pass. The winter may . . . pass. The Academy . . . a picture in very bright colours . . . a woman sitting by the roadside with a shawl round her shoulders and a red skirt and red cheeks and bright green country behind her . . . people moving about on the shiny floor, someone just behind saying, "that is plein-air, these are the plein-airistes"--the woman in the picture was like the housekeeper. . . .

A brilliant light flashed into the room . . . lightning--how strange the room looked--the screens had been moved--the walls and corners and little beds had looked like daylight. Someone was talking across the landing. Emma was awake. Another flash came and movements and cries. Emma screamed aloud, sitting up in bed. "Ach Gott! Clara! *Clara!*" she screamed. Cries came from the next room. A match was struck across the landing and voices sounded. Gertrude was in the room lighting the gas and Clara tugging down the blind. Emma was sitting with her hands pressed to her eyes, quickly gasping, "Ach Clara! Mein Gott! Ach Gott!" On Ulrica's bed nothing was visible but a mound of bedclothes. The whole landing was astir. Fraulein's voice called up urgently from below.

### 10

Miriam was the last to reach the schoolroom. The girls were drawn up on either side of the gaslit room--leaving the shuttered windows clear. She moved to take a chair at the end of the table in front of the saal doors. "Na!" said Fraulein sharply from the sofa-corner. "Not there! In full current!" Her voice shook. Miriam drew the chair to the end of the room of figures and sat down next to Solomon Martin. The wind rushed through the garden, the thunder rattled across the sky. "Oh, Clara! Fraulein! Nein!" gasped Emma. She was sitting opposite, between Clara and Jimmie with flushed face and eyes strained wide, twisting her linked hands against her knees. Jimmie patted her wrist, "It's all right, Emmchen," she muttered cheerfully. "Nein, Christina!" jerked Fraulein sharply. "I will not have that! To touch the flesh! You understand, all! That you know. All! Such immodesty!"

Miriam leaned forward and glanced. Fraulein was sitting very upright on the sofa in a shapeless black cloak with her hands clasped on her breast. Near her was Ulrica in her trailing white dressing-gown, her face pressed against the back of the sofa. In the far corner, the other side of Fraulein sat Gertrude in her grey ulster, her knees comfortably crossed, a quilted scarlet silk bedroom-slipper sticking out under the hem of her ulster.

The thunder crashed and pounded just above them. Everyone started and ex-claimed. Emma flung her arms up across her face and sat back in her chair with a hooting cry. From the sofa came a hidden sobbing and gasping. "Ach Himmel! Ach Herr *Je*sus! Ach du *lie*-ber, *lie*-ber Gott!"

Miriam wished they could see the lightning and be prepared for the crashes. If she were alone she would watch for the flashes and put her fingers in her ears after each flash. The shock of the sound was intolerable to her. Once it had broken, she drank in the tumult joyfully. She sat tense and miserable longing to get to bed. She wondered whether it would be of any use to explain to Fraulein that they would be safer in their iron bedsteads than anywhere in the house. She tried to distract her thoughts. . . . Fancy Jimmie's name being Christina. . . . It suited her exactly sitting there in her little striped dressing-gown with its "toby" frill. How Harriett would scream if she could see them all sitting round. But she and Harriett had once lain very quiet and frightened in a storm by the sea--the thunder and lightning had come together and someone had looked in and said, "There won't be another like that, children." "My boots, I should hope not," Harriett had said.

For a while it seemed as though cannon balls were being thumped down and rumbled about on the floor above; then came another deafening crash. Jimmie laughed and put up her hand to her loosely-pinned top-knot as if to see whether it was still there. Outcries came from all over the room. After the first shock which had made her sit up sharply and draw herself convulsively together, Miriam found herself turning towards Solomon Martin who had also stirred and sat forward. Their eyes met full and consulted. Solomon's lips were compressed, her perspiring face was alight and determined. Miriam felt that she looked for long into those steady, oily half-smiling brown eyes. When they both relaxed she sat back, catch-ing a sympathetic challenging flash from Gertrude. She drew a deep breath and felt proud and easy. Let it bang, she said to herself. I must think of doors suddenly banging--that never makes me jumpy--and she sat easily breathing.

Fraulein had said something in German in a panting voice, and Bertha had stood up and said, "I'll get the Bible, Fraulein."

"Ei! Bewahre! Ber *tha!*" shouted Clara. "Stay only here! Stay only here!"

"Nein, Bertha, nein, mein Kind," moaned Fraulein sadly.

"It's really perfectly all right, Fraulein," said Bertha, getting quietly to the door.

As Fraulein opened the great book on her knees the rain hissed down into the garden.

"Gott sei Dank," she said, in a clear childlike voice. "It dot besser wenn da regnet?" enquired the housekeeper, looking round the room. She began vigorously wiping her face and neck with the skirt of the short cotton jacket she wore over her red petticoat.

Ulrica broke into steady weeping.

Fraulein read Psalms, ejaculating the short phrases as if they were petitions, with a pause between each. When the thunder came she raised her voice against it and read more rapidly.

As the storm began to abate a little party of English went to the kitchen and brought back milk and biscuits and jam.

## 11

"You will be asleep, Miss Hendershon." Miriam started at the sound of Ulrica's wailing whisper. Fraulein had only just gone. She had been sitting on the end of Emma's bed talking quietly of self-control and now Emma was asleep. Ulrica's corner had been perfectly quiet. Miriam had been lying listening to the steady swishing of the rain against the chestnut leaves.

"No; what is it?"

"Oh, most wonderful. Ich bin so empfindlich. I am so sensible."

"Sensitive?"

"Oh, it was most wonderful. Only hear and I shall tell you. This evening when the storm leave himself down it was exactly as my Konfirmation."

"Yes."

"It was as my Konfirmation. I think of that wonderful day, my white dress, the flower-bouquet and how I weeped always. Oh, it was all of most beautifullest. I am so sensible."

"Oh, yes," whispered Miriam.

"I weeped so! All day I have weeped! The all whole day! And my mozzer she console me I shall not weep.  And I weep.  Ach!  It was of most beautifullest."

Miriam felt as if she were being robbed. . . . This was Ulrica.  "You remember the Konfirmation, miss?"

"Oh, I remember."

"Have you weeped?"

"We say *cry,* not weep, except in poetry--weinen, to cry."

"Have you cry?"

"No, I didn't cry.  But we mustn't talk.  We must go to sleep.  Good night."

"Gute Nacht.  Ach, wie empfindlich bin ich, wie empfindlich. . . ."

Miriam lay thinking of how she and Harriett on their confirmation morning had met the vicar in the Upper Richmond Road, having gone out, contrary to the desire expressed by him at his last preparation class, and how he had stopped and greeted them.  She had tried to look vague and sad and to murmur something in spite of the bull's-eye in her cheek and had suddenly noticed as they stood grouped that Harriett's little sugar-loaf hat was askew and her brown eye underneath it was glaring fixedly at the vicar above the little knob in her cheek--and how they some-how got away and went, gently reeling and colliding, moaning and gasping down the road out of hearing.

12

Early next morning Judy came in to tell Emma and Ulrica to get up at once and come and help the housekeeper make the rooms tidy and prepare breakfast.  Miriam lay motionless while Emma unfolded and arranged the screens.  Then she gazed at the ceiling.  It was pleasant to lie tranquil, open-eyed and unchallenged while others moved busily about.  Two separate, sudden and resounding garglings almost startled her to thought, but she resisted, and presently she was alone in the strange room.  She supposed it must be cooler after the storm.  She felt strong and languid.  She could feel the shape and weight of each limb; sounds came to her with perfect distinctness; the sounds downstairs and a low-voiced conversation across the landing, little faint marks that human beings were making on the great wide stillness, the stillness that brooded along her white ceiling and all round her and right out through the world; the faint scent of her soap-tablet reached her from the distant wash-stand. She felt that her short sleep must have been perfect, that it had carried her down and down into the heart of tranquillity where she still lay awake, and drinking as if at a source. Cool streams seemed to be flowing in her brain, through her heart, through every vein, her breath was like a live cool stream flowing through her.

She remembered that she had dreamed her favourite dream--floating through clouds and above treetops and villages. She had almost brushed the treetops, that had been the happiest moment, and had caught sight of a circular seat round the trunk of a large old tree and a group of white cottages.

She stirred; her hands seemed warm on her cool chest and the warmth of her body sent up a faint pleasant sense of personality. "It's me," she said, and smiled.

"Look here, you'd better get up, my dear," she murmured.

She wanted to have the whole world in and be reconciled. But she knew that if anyone came, she would contract and the expression of her face would change and they would hate her or be indifferent. She knew that if she even moved she would be changed.

"Get up."

She listened for a while to two voices across the landing. Millie's thick and plaintive with her hay-fever and Bertha's thin and cold and level and reassuring. . . . Bertha's voice was like the morning, clean and cool. . . . Then she got up and shut the door.

The sky was a vivid grey--against its dark background the tops of heavy masses of cloud were standing up just above the roof-line of the houses beyond the neighbouring gardens. The trees and the grey roofs and the faces of the houses were staringly bright. They were absolutely stiff, nothing was moving, there were no shadows.

A soft distant rumble of thunder came as she was dressing. . . . The storm was still going on . . . what an extraordinary time of day for thunder . . . the excitement was not over . . . they were still a besieged party . . . all staying at the Bienenkorb together. . . . How beautiful it sounded rumbling away over the country in the morning. When she had finished struggling with her long thick hair and put the hairpins into the solid coil on the top of her head and tied the stout doubled door-knocker plait at her neck, she put on the rose-madder blouse. The mirror was lower and twice as large as the one in the garret, larger than the one she had shared with Har-riett. "How jolly I look," she thought, "jolly and big somehow. Mother would like me this morning. I *am* German-looking to-day, pinky red and yellow hair. But I haven't got a German expression and I don't smile like a German. . . . She smiled. . . . Silly, baby-face! Doll! Never mind! I look jolly. She looked gravely into her eyes. . . . There's something about my expression." Her face grew wistful. "It isn't vain to like it. It's something. It isn't me. It's something I am, somehow. Oh, *do* stay," she said, "do be like that always." She sighed and turned away saying in Harriett's voice, "Oo--crumbs! This is no place for *me.*"

## 13

The sky seen from the summer-house was darker still. There were no massed clouds, nothing but a hard even dark copper-grey, and away through the gap the distant country was bright like a little painted scene. On the horizon the hard dark sky shut down. At intervals thunder rumbled evenly, far away. Miriam stood still in the middle of the summer-house floor. It was half-dark; the morning saal lay in a hot sultry twilight. The air in the summer-house was heavy and damp. She stood with her half-closed hands gathered against her. "How perfectly magnificent," she murmured, gazing out through the hard half-darkness to where the brightly coloured world lay in a strip and ended on the hard sky.

"Yes . . . yes," came a sad low voice at her side.

For a second Miriam did not turn. She drank in the quiet "yes, yes," the hard fixed scene seemed to move. Who loved it too, the dark sky and the storm? Then she focussed her companion who was standing a little behind her, and gazed at Fraulein; she hardly saw her, she seemed still to see the outdoor picture. Fraulein made a movement towards her; and then she saw for a moment the strange grave young look in her eyes. Fraulein had looked at her in that moment as an equal. It was as if they had embraced each other.

Then Fraulein said sadly, "You like the storm-weather, Miss Henderson."

"Yes."

Fraulein sighed, looking out across the country. "We are in the hollow of His Hand," she murmured. "Come to your breakfast, my child," she chided, smiling.

## 14

There was no church. Late in the afternoon when the sky lifted they all went to the woods in their summer dresses and hats. They had permission to carry their gloves and Elsa Speier's parasol and lace scarf hung from her wrist. The sky was growing higher and lighter, but there was no sun. They entered the dark woods by a little well-swept pathway and for a while there was a strip of sky above their heads; but presently the trees grew tall and dense, the sky was shut out and their footsteps and voices began to echo about them as they straggled along, grouping and regrouping as the pathway widened and narrowed, gathering their skirts clear of the wet undergrowth. They crossed a roadway and two carriage loads of men and women talking and laughing and shouting with shining red faces passed swiftly by, one close behind the other. Beyond the roadway the great trees towered up in a sort of twilight. There were no flowers here, but bright fungi shone here and there about the roots of the trees and they all stood for a moment to listen to the tinkling of a little stream.

Pathways led away in all directions. It was growing lighter. There were faint chequers of light and shade about them as they walked. The forest was growing golden all round them, lifting and opening, gold and green, clearer and clearer. There were bright jewelled patches in amongst the trees; the boles of the trees shone out sharp grey and silver and flaked with sharp green leaves away and away until they melted into a mist of leafage. Singing sounded suddenly away in the wood; a sudden strong shouting of men's voices singing together like one voice in four parts, four shouts in one sound.

"O *Sonn*enschein! O *Sonn*enschein!"

Between the two exclamatory shouts, the echo rang through the woods and the listening girls heard the sharp drip, drip and murmur of the little stream near by, then the voices swung on into the song, strongly interwoven, swelling and lifting; dropping to a soft even staccato and swelling strongly out again.

"Wie scheinst du mir in's Herz hinein Weck'st drinnen lauter Liebeslust, Dass mir so enge wird die Brust O *Sonn*enschein! O *Sonn*---enschein!"

When the voices ceased there was a faint distant sound of crackling twigs and the echo of talking and laughter.

"Ach Studenten!"

"Irgend ein Mannergesangverein."

"I think we ought to get back, Gertrude. Fraulein *said* only an hour altogether and it's church tonight."

"We'll get back, Millenium mine--never fear."

As they began to retrace their steps Clara softly sang the last line of the song, the highest note ringing, faint and clear, away into the wood.

"Ho-lah!" A mighty answering shout rang through the wood. It was like a word of command.

"Oh, come along home; Clara, what are you dreaming of?"

"Taisez-vous, taisez-vous, Clarah!" C'est honteux mon Dieu!"

# CHAPTER IX

## 1

The next afternoon they all drove in a high wide brake with an awning, five miles out into the country to have tea at a forest-inn. The inn appeared at last standing back from the wide roadway along which they had come, creamy-white and grey-roofed, long and low and with overhanging eaves, close against the forest. They pulled up and Pastor Lahmann dropped the steps and got out. Miriam who was sitting next to the door felt that the long sitting in two rows confronted in the hard afternoon light, bumped and shaken and teased with the crunchings and slitherings of the wheels the grinding and squeaking of the brake, had made them all enemies. She had sat tense and averted, seeing the general greenery, feeling that the cool flowing air might be great happiness, conscious of each form and each voice, of the insincerity of the exclamations and the babble of conversation that struggled above the noise of their going, half seeing Pastor Lahmann opposite to her, a little insincerely smiling man in an alpaca suit and a soft felt hat. She got down the steps without his assistance. With whom should she take refuge? . . . no Minna. There were long tables and little round tables standing about under the trees in front of the inn. Some students in Polytechnik uniform were leaning out of an upper window.

The landlord came out. Everyone was out of the brake and standing about. Tall Fraulein was taking short padding steps towards the inn-door. A strong grip came on Miriam's arm and she was propelled rapidly along towards the farther greenery. Gertrude was talking to her in loud rallying tones, asking questions in German and answering them herself. Miriam glanced round at her face. It was crimson and quivering with laughter. The strong laughter and her strong features seemed to hide the peculiar roughness of her skin and coarseness of her hair. They made the round of one of the long tables. When they were on the far side Gertrude said, "I think you'll see a friend of mine to-day, Henderson."

"D'you mean Erica's brother?"

"There's his chum anyhow at yondah window."

"Oh, I say."

"Hah! Spree, eh? Happy thought of Lily's to bring us here."

Miriam pondered, distressed. "You must tell me which it is if we see him."

Their party was taking possession of a long table near by. Returning to her voluble talk, Gertrude steered Miriam towards them.

As they settled round the table under the quiet trees the first part of the waltz movement of Weber's "Invitation" sounded out through the upper window. The brilliant tuneless passages bounding singly up the piano, flowing down entwined, were shaped by an iron rhythm.

Everyone stirred. Smiles broke. Fraulein lifted her head until her chin was high, smiled slowly until the fullest width was reached and made a little chiding sound in her throat.

Pastor Lahmann laughed with raised eyebrows. "Ah! la valse . . . les etudiants."

The window was empty. The assault settled into a gently-leaping, heavily-thudding waltz.

As the waiter finished clattering down a circle of cups and saucers in front of Fraulein, the unseen iron hands dropped tenderly into the central melody of the waltz. The notes no longer bounded and leaped but went dreaming along in an even slow swinging movement.

It seemed to Miriam that the sound of a far-off sea was in them, and the wind and the movement of distant trees and the shedding and pouring of faraway moonlight. One by one, delicately and quietly the young men's voices dropped in, and the sea and the wind and the trees and the pouring moonlight came near.

When the music ceased Miriam hoped she had not been gazing at the window. It frightened and disgusted her to see that all the girls seemed to be sitting up and . . . being bright . . . affected. She could hardly believe it. She flushed with shame. . . . Fast, horrid . . . perfect strangers . . . it was terrible . . . it spoilt everything. Sitting up like that and grimacing. . . . It was different for Gertrude. How happy Gertrude must be. She was sitting with her elbows on the table laughing out across the table about something. . . . Millie was not being horrid. She looked just as usual, pudgy and babyish and surprised and half resentful . . . it was her eyebrows. Miriam began looking at eyebrows.

There was a sudden silence all round the table. Standing at Fraulein's side was a young student holding his peaked cap in his hand and bowing with downcast eyes. Above his pallid scarred face his hair stood upright. He bowed at the end of each phrase. Miriam's heart bounded in anticipation. Would Fraulein let them dance after tea, on the grass?

But Fraulein with many smiles and kind words denied the young man's formally repeated pleadings. They finished tea to the strains of a funeral march.

2

They were driving swiftly along through the twilight. The warm scents of the woods stood across the roadway. They breathed them in. Sitting at the forward end of the brake, Miriam could turn and see the shining of the road and the edges of the high woods.

Underneath the awning, faces were growing dim. Warm at her side was Emma. Emma's hand was on her arm under a mass of fern and grasses. Voices quivered and laughed. Miriam looked again and again at Pastor Lahmann sitting almost opposite to her, next to Fraulein Pfaff. She could look at him more easily than at either of the girls. She felt that only he could feel the beauty of the evening exactly as she did. Several times she met and quietly contemplated his dark eyes. She felt that there was someone in those eyes who was neither tiresome nor tame. She was looking at someone to whom those boys and that dead wife were nothing. At first he had met her eyes formally, then with obvious embarrassment, and at last simply and gravely.

She felt easy and happy in this communion. Dimly she was conscious that it sustained her, it gave her dignity and poise. She thought that its meaning must, if she observed it at all, be quite obvious to Fraulein and must reveal her to her. Presently her eyes were drawn to meet Fraulein's and she read there a disgust and a loathing such as she had never seen. The woods receded, the beauty dropped out of them. The crunching of the wheels sounded out suddenly. What was the good of the brake-load of grimacing people? Miriam wanted to stop it and get out and stroll home along the edge of the wood with the quiet man.

"Haben die Damen veilleicht ein Rad verloren?"

A deep voice on the steps of the brake. . . . "Have the ladies lost a wheel, perhaps?" Miriam translated helplessly to herself during a general outbreak of laughter. . . .

In a moment a brake overtook them and drove alongside in the twilight. The drivers whipped up their horses. The two vehicles raced and rumbled along keeping close together. Fraulein called to their driver to desist. The students slackened down too and began singing at random, one against the other; those on the near side standing up and bowing and laughing. A bouquet of fern fronds came in over Judy's head, missing the awning and falling against Clara's knees. She rose and flung it back and then everyone seemed to be standing up and laughing and throwing.

They drove home, slowly, side by side, shouting and singing and throwing. Warm, blinding masses of fragrant grass came from the students' brake and were thrown to and fro through the darkness lit by the lamps of the two carriages.

# CHAPTER X

## 1

Towards the end of June there were frequent excursions.

Into all the gatherings at Waldstrasse the outside world came like a presence. It removed the sense of pressure, of being confronted and challenged. Everything that was said seemed to be incidental to it, like remarks dropped in a low tone between individuals at a great conference.

Miriam wondered again and again whether her companions shared this sense with her. Sometimes when they were all sitting together she longed to ask, to find out, to get some public acknowledgment of the magic that lay over everything. At times it seemed as if could they all be still for a moment--it must take shape. It was everywhere, in the food, in the fragrance rising from the opened lid of the tea-urn, in all the needful unquestioned movements, the requests, the handings and thanks, the going from room to room, the partings and assemblings. It hung about the fabrics and fittings of the house. Overwhelmingly it came in through oblongs of window giving on to stairways. Going upstairs in the light pouring in from some uncurtained window, she would cease for a moment to breathe.

Whenever she found herself alone she began to sing, softly. When she was with others a head drooped or lifted, the movement of a hand, the light falling along the detail of a profile could fill her with happiness.

It made companionship a perpetual question. At rare moments there would come a tingling from head to foot, a faint buzzing at her lips and at the tip of each finger. At these moments she could raise her eyes calmly to those about her and drink in the fact of their presence, see them all with perfect distinctness, but without distinguishing one from the other. She wanted to say, "Isn't it extraordinary?

Do you realise?" She felt that if only she could make her meaning clear all difficulties must vanish. Outside in the open, going forward to some goal through
sunny mornings, gathering at inns, wading through the scented undergrowth of the
woods, she would dream of the secure return to Waldstrasse, their own beleaguered
place. She saw it opening out warm and familiar back and back to the strange beginning in the winter. They would be there again to-night, singing.

2

One morning she knew that there was going to be a change. The term was
coming to an end. There was to be a going away. The girls were talking about
"Norderney."

"Going to Norderney, Hendy?" Jimmie said suddenly.

"Ah!" she responded mysteriously. For the rest of that day she sat contracted
and fearful.

3

"You shall write and enquire of your good parents what they would have you
do. You shall tell them that the German pupils return all to their homes; that the
English pupils go for a happy holiday to the sea."

"Oh yes," said Miriam conversationally, with trembling breath.

"It is of course evident that since you will have no duties to perform, I cannot
support the expense of your travelling and your maintenance."

"Oh no, of course not," said Miriam, her hands pressed against her knee.

She sat shivering in the warm dim saal shaded by the close sun-blinds. It looked
as she had seen it with her father for the first time and Fraulein sitting near seemed
to be once more in the heavy panniered, blue velvet dress.

She waited stiff and ugly till Fraulein, secure and summer-clad, spoke softly
again.

"You think, my child, you shall like the profession of a teacher?"

"Oh yes," said Miriam, from the midst of a tingling flush.

"I think you have many qualities that make the teacher. . . . You are earnest and serious-minded. . . . Grave. . . . Sometimes perhaps overgrave for your years. . . . But you have a serious fault--which must be corrected if you wish to succeed in your calling."

Miriam tried to pull her features into an easy enquiring seriousness. A darkness was threatening her. "You have a most unfortunate manner."

Without relaxing, Miriam quivered. She felt the blood mount to her head.

"You must adopt a quite, quite different manner. Your influence is, I think, good, a good English influence in its most general effect. But it is too slightly so and of too much indirection. You must exert it yourself, in a manner more alive, you must make it your aim that you shall have a responsible influence, a direct personal influence. You have too much of chill and formality. It makes a stiffness that I am willing to believe you do not intend."

Miriam felt a faint dizziness.

"If you should fail to become more genial, more simple and natural as to your bearing, you will neither make yourself understood nor will you be loved by your pupils."

"No--" responded Miriam, assuming an air of puzzled and interested consideration of Fraulein's words. She was recovering. She must get to the end of the interview and get away and find the answer. Far away beneath her fear and indignation, Fraulein was answered. She must get away and say the answer to herself.

"To truly fulfil the most serious rôle of the teacher you must enter into the personality of each pupil and must sympathise with the struggles of each one upon the path on which our feet are set. Efforts to good kindliness and thought for others must be encouraged. The teacher shall he sunshine, human sunshine, encouraging all effort and all lovely things in the personality of the pupil."

Fraulein rose and stood, tall. Then her half-tottering decorous footsteps began. Miriam had hardly listened to her last words. She felt tears of anger rising and tried to smile.

"I shall say now no more. But when you shall hear from your good parents, we can further discuss our plans." Fraulein was at the door.

Fraulein left the saal by the small door and Miriam felt her way to the schoolroom. The girls were gathering there ready for a walk. Some were in the hall and Fraulein's voice was giving instructions: "Machen Sie schnell, Miss Henderson," she called.

Fraulein had never before called to her like that. It had always been as if she did not see her but assumed her ready to fall in with the general movements.

Now it was Fraulein calling to her as she might do to Gertrude or Solomon. There was no hurried whisper from Jimmie telling her to "fly for her life."

"Ja, Fraulein," she cried gaily and blundered towards the basement stairs. Mademoiselle was standing averted at the head of them; Miriam glanced at her. Her face was red and swollen with crying.

The sight amazed Miriam. She considered the swollen suffusion under the large black hat as she ran downstairs. She hoped Mademoiselle did not see her glance. . . . Mademoiselle, standing there all disfigured and blotchy about something . . . it was nothing . . . it couldn't be anything. . . . If anyone were dead she would not be standing there . . . it was just some silly prim French quirk . . . her dignity . . . someone had been "grossiere" . . . and there she stood in her black hat and black cotton gloves. . . . Hurriedly putting on her hat and long lace scarf she decided that she would not change her shoes. Somewhere out in the sunshine a hurdy-gurdy piped out the air of "Dass du mich liebst das wusst ich." She glanced at the frosted barred window through which the dim light came into the dressing-room. The piping notes, out of tune, wrongly emphasised, slurring one into the other, followed her across the dark basement hall and came faintly to her as she went slowly upstairs. There was no hurry. Everyone was talking busily in the hall, drowning the sound of her footsteps. She had forgotten her gloves. She went back into the cool grey musty rooms. A little crack in an upper pane shone like a gold thread. The barrel-organ piped. As she stooped to gather up her gloves from the floor she felt the cold stone firm and secure under her hand. And the house stood up all round her with its rooms and the light lying along stairways and passages, and outside the bright hot sunshine and the roadways leading in all directions, out into Germany.

How could Fraulein possibly think she could afford to go to Norderney? They would all go. Things would go on. She could not go there--nor back to England. It was cruel . . . just torture and worry again . . . with the bright house all round her-- the high rooms, the dark old pianos, strange old garret, the unopened door beyond it. No help anywhere.

## 4

As they walked she laughed and talked with the girls, responding excitedly to all that was said.  They walked along a broad and almost empty boulevard in two rows of four and five abreast, with Mademoiselle and Judy bringing up the rear.  The talk was general and there was much laughter.  It was the kind of interchange that arose when they were all together and there was anything "in the air," the kind that Miriam most disliked.  She joined in it feverishly.  It's perfectly natural that they should all be excited about the holidays she told herself, stifling her thoughts.  But it must not go too far.  They wanted to be jolly. . . . If I could be jolly too they would like me.  I must not be a wet blanket. . . . Mademoiselle's voice was not heard.  Miriam felt that the steering of the conversation might fall to anyone.  Mademoiselle was extinguished.  She must exert her influence.  Presently she forgot Mademoiselle's presence altogether.  They were all walking along very quickly. . . . If she were going to Norderney with the English girls she must be on easy terms with them.

"Ah, ha!" somebody was saying.

"Oh-ho!" said Miriam in response.

"Ih-hi!" came another voice.

"Tre-la-la," trilled Bertha Martin gently.

"You mean Turrah-lahee-tee," said Miriam.

"Good for you, Hendy," blared Gertrude, in a swinging middle tone.

"Chalk it up.  Chalk it up, children," giggled Jimmie.

Millie looked pensively about her with vague disapproval.  Her eyebrows were up.  It seemed as if anything might happen; as if at any moment they might all begin running in different directions.

"*Cave,* my dear brats, be artig," came Bertha's cool even tones.

"Ah! we are observed."

"No, we are not observed.  The observer observeth not."

Miriam saw her companions looking across the boulevard.

Following their eyes she found the figure of Pastor Lahmann walking swiftly bag in hand in the direction of an opening into a side street.

"Ah!" she cried gaily. "Voila Monsieur; courrez, Mademoiselle!"

At once she felt that it was cruel to draw attention to Mademoiselle when she was dumpy and upset.

"What a fool I am," she moaned in her mind. 'Why can't I say the right thing?"

"Ce n'est pas moi," said Mademoiselle, "qui fait les avanses."

The group walked on for a moment or two in silence. Bertha Martin was swinging her left foot out across the curb with each step, giving her right heel a little twirl to keep her balance.

"You are very clever, Bair-ta," said Mademoiselle, still in French, "but you will never make a prima ballerina."

"Hulloh!" breathed Jimmie, "she's perking up."

"Isn't she?" said Miriam, feeling that she was throwing away the last shred of her dignity.

"What was the matter?" she continued, trying to escape from her confusion.

Mademoiselle's instant response to her cry at the sight of Pastor Lahmann rang in her ears. She blushed to the soles of her feet. . . . How could Mademoiselle misunderstand her insane remark? What did she mean? What did she really think of her? Just kind old Lahmann--walking along there in the outside world. . . . *She* did not want to stop him. . . . He was a sort of kinsman for Mademoiselle . . . that was what she had meant. Oh, why couldn't she get away from all these girls? . . . indeed--and again she saw the hurrying figure which had disappeared leaving the boulevard with its usual effect of a great strange ocean--he could have brought help and comfort to all of them if he had seen them and stopped. Pastor Lahmann--Lahmann--perhaps she would not see him again. Perhaps he could tell her what she ought to do.

"Oh, my dear," Jimmie was saying, "didn't you know?--a fearful row."

Mademoiselle's laughter tinkled out from the rear.

"A row?"

"Fearful!" Jimmie's face came round, round-eyed under her white sailor hat that sat slightly tilted on the peak of her hair.

"What about?"

"Something about a letter or something, or some letters or something--I don't know. Something she took out of the letter-box, it was unlocked or something and Ulrica saw her *and told Lily!*"

"Goodness!" breathed Miriam.

"Yes, and Lily had her in her room and Ulrica and poor little Petite couldn't deny it. Ulrica said she did nothing but cry and cry. She's been crying all the morning, poor little pig."

"Why did she want to take anything out of the box?"

"Oh, I don't know. There was a fearful row anyhow. Ulrica said Lily talked like a clergyman--wie ein Pfarrer. . . . I don't know. Ulrica said she was *opening* a letter. *I* don't know."

"But she can't read German or English."

"*I* don't know. Ask me another."

"It is *extraordinary.*"

"What's extraordinary?" asked Bertha from the far side of Jimmie.

"Petite and that letter."

"Oh."

"What did the Kiddy *want?*"

"Oh, my dear, don't ask me to explain the peculiarities of the French temperament."

"Yes, but all the letters in the letter-box would be English or German, as Hendy says."

Bertha glanced at Miriam. Miriam flushed. She could not discuss Mademoiselle with two of the girls at once.

"Rum go," said Bertha.

"You're right, my son. It's rum. It's all over now, anyhow. There's no accounting for tastes. Poor old Petite."


5


Miriam woke in the moonlight. She saw Mademoiselle's face as it had looked at tea-time, pale and cruel, silent and very old. Someone had said she had been in Fraulein's room again all the afternoon. . . . Fraulein had spoken to her once or twice during tea. She had answered coolly and eagerly . . . disgusting . . . like a child that had been whipped and forgiven. . . . How could Fraulein dare to forgive anybody?

She lay motionless. The night was cool. The screens had not been moved. She felt that the door was shut. After a while she began in imagination a conversation with Eve.

"You see the trouble *was,*" she said and saw Eve's downcast believing admiring sympathetic face, "Fraulein talked to me about manner, she simply wanted me to grimace, *simply.  You* know--be like other people."

Eve laughed. "Yes, I know."

"You see? *Simply.*"

"Well, if you wanted to stay, why couldn't you?"

"I simply couldn't; you know how people are."

"But you can act so splendidly."

"But you can't keep it up."

"Why not?"

*"Eve.* There you are, you see, you always go back."

"I mean I think it would be simply lovely. If I were clever like you I should do it all the time, be simply always gushing and 'charming'."

Then she reminded Eve of the day they had walked up the lane to the Heath talking over all the manners they would like to have--and how Sarah suddenly in the middle of supper had caricatured the one they had chosen. "Of course you overdid it," she concluded, and Eve crimsoned and said, "Oh yes, I know it was my fault. But you could have begun all over again in Germany and been quite different."

"Yes, I know I thought about that. . . . But if you knew as much of the world as I do. . . ."

Eve stared, showing a faint resentment.

Miriam thought of Eve's many suitors, of her six months' betrothal, of her lifelong peacemaking, her experiment in being governess to the two children of an artist--a little green-robed boy threatening her with a knife.

"Yes, but I mean if you had been about."

"I know," smiled Eve confidently. "You mean if I were you. Go on. I know. Explain, old thing."

"Well, I mean of course if you are a governess in a school you *can't* be jolly and charming. You can't be idiotic or anything. . . . I did think about it. Don't tell anybody. But I thought for a little while I might go into a family--one of the girls' families--the German girls, and begin having a German manner. Two of the girls asked me. One of them was ill and went away--that Pomeranian one I told you about. Well, then, I didn't tell you about that little one and her sister--they asked me to go to them for the holidays. The youngest said--it was *so* absurd--'you shall marry my bruzzer--he is mairchant--very welty'--absurd."

"*Not* absurd--you probably *would* have, away from that school."

"D'you think so?"

"Yes, you would have been a regular German, fat and jolly and laughing."

"I know. My dear, I thought about it. You may imagine. I wondered if I ought."

"Why didn't you try?"

Why not? Why was she not going to try? Eve would, she was sure in her place. . . .

Why not grimace and be very "bright" and "animated" until the end of the term and then go and stay with the Bergmanns for two months and be as charming as she could? . . . Her heart sank. . . . She imagined a house, everyone kind and blond and smiling. Emma's big tall brother smiling and joking and liking her. She would laugh and pretend and flirt like the Pooles and make up to him--and it would be lovely for a little while. Then she would offend someone. She would offend everyone but Emma--and get tired and cross and lose her temper. Stare at them all as they said the things everybody said, the things she hated; and she would sit glowering, and suddenly refuse to allow the women to be familiar with her. . . . She tried to see the brother more clearly. She looked at the screen. The Bergmanns' house would be full of German furniture. . . . At the end of a week every bit of it would reproach her.

She tried to imagine him without the house and the family, not talking or joking or pretending . . . alone and sad . . . despising his family . . . needing her. He loved forests and music. He had a great strong solid voice and was strong and sure about everything and she need never worry any more.

"Seit ich ihn gesehen  Glaub' ich blind zu sein."

There would be a garden and German springs and summers and sunsets and

strong kind arms and a shoulder. She would grow so happy. No one would recognise her as the same person. She would wear a band of turquoise-blue velvet ribbon
round her hair and look at the mountains. . . . No good. She could never get out to
that. Never. She could not pretend long enough. Everything would be at an end
long before there was any chance of her turning into a happy German woman.

Certainly with a German man she would be angry at once. She thought of the
men she had seen--in the streets, in cafes and gardens, the masters in the school,
photographs in the girls' albums. They had all offended her at once. Something in
their bearing and manner. . . . Blind and impudent. . . . She thought of the interview
she had witnessed between Ulrica and her cousin--the cousin coming up from the
estate in Erfurth, arriving in a carriage, Fraulein's manner, her smiles and hints;
Ulrica standing in the saal in her sprigged saffron muslin dress curtseying . . . with
bent head, the cousin's condescending laughing voice. It would never do for her to
go into a German home. She must not say anything about the chance of going to
the Bergmanns'--even to Eve.

She imagined Eve sitting listening in the window space in the bow that was
carpeted with linoleum to look like parquet flooring. Beyond them lay the length
of the Turkey carpet darkening away under the long table. She could see each object on the shining sideboard. The silver biscuit-box and the large epergne made
her feel guilty and shifting, guilty from the beginning of things.

"You see, Eve, I thought counting it all up that if I came home it would cost
less than going to Norderney and that all the expense of my going to Germany and
coming back is less than what it would have cost to keep me at home for the five
months I've been there--I wish you'd tell everybody that."

6

She turned about in bed; her head was growing fevered.
She conjured up a vision of the backs of the books in the bookcase in the dining-room at home. . . . Iliad and Odyssey . . . people going over the sea in boats and
someone doing embroidery . . . that little picture of Hector and Andromache in the
corner of a page . . . he in armour . . . she, in a trailing dress, holding up her baby.
Both, silly. . . . She wished she had read more carefully. She could not remember

anything in Lecky or Darwin that would tell her what to do . . . Hudibras . . . The Atomic Theory . . . Ballads and Poems, D. G. Rossetti . . . Kinglake's Crimea . . . Palgrave's Arabia . . . Crimea. . . . The Crimea. . . . Florence Nightingale; a picture somewhere; a refined face, with cap and strings. . . . She must have smiled. . . . Motley's Rise of . . . Rise of . . . Motley's Rise of the Dutch Republic. . . . Motley's Rise of the Dutch Republic and the Chronicles of the Schonberg-Cotta family. She held to the memory of these two books. Something was coming from them to her. She handled the shiny brown gold-tooled back of Motley's Rise and felt the hard graining of the red-bound Chronicles. . . . There were green trees outside in the moonlight . . . in Luther's Germany . . . trees and fields and German towns and then Holland. She breathed more easily. Her eyes opened serenely. Tranquil moonlight lay across the room. It surprised her like a sudden hand stroking her brow. It seemed to feel for her heart. If she gave way to it her thoughts would go. Perhaps she ought to watch it and let her thoughts go. It passed over her trouble like her mother did when she said, "Don't go so deeply into everything, chickie. You must learn to take life as it comes. Ah-eh if I were strong I could show you how to enjoy life. . . ." Delicate little mother, running quickly downstairs clearing her throat to sing. But mother did not know. She had no reasoning power. She could not help because she did not know. The moonlight was sad and hesitating. Miriam closed her eyes again. Luther . . . pinning up that notice on a church door. . . . (Why is Luther like a dyspeptic blackbird? Because the Diet of Worms did not agree with him) . . . and then leaving the notice on the church door and going home to tea . . . coffee . . . some evening meal . . . Kathe . . . Kathe . . . happy Kathe. . . . They pinned up that notice on a Roman Catholic church . . . and all the priests looked at them . . . and behind the priests were torture and dark places . . . Luther looking up to God . . . saying you couldn't get away from your sins by paying money . . . standing out in the world and Kathe making the meal at home . . . Luther was fat and German. Perhaps his face perspired . . . Eine feste Burg; a firm fortress . . . a round tower made of old brown bricks and no windows. . . . No need for Kathe to smile. . . . She had been a nun . . . and then making a lamplit meal for Lather in a wooden German house . . . and Rome waiting to kill them.

Darwin had come since then. There were people . . . distinguished minds, who thought Darwin was true.

No God.  No Creation.  The struggle for existence.  Fighting. . . . Fighting. . . . Fighting. . . . Everybody groping and fighting. . . . Fraulein. . . . Some said it was true . . . some not.  They could not both be right.  It was probably true . . . only old-fashioned people thought it was not.  It was true.  Just that--monkeys fighting.  But who began it?  Who made Fraulein?  Tough leathery monkey. . . .

7

Then nothing matters.  Just one little short life. . . .

"A few more years shall roll . . .  A few more seasons pass. . . ."

There was a better one than that . . . not so organ-grindery.

"Swift to its close ebbs out life's little day;  Earth's joys grow dim, its glories fade away;  Change and decay in all around I see."

Wow-wow-wow-whiney-caterwauley. . . .

Mr. Brough quoted Milton in a sermon and said he was a materialist. . . . Pater said it was a bold thing to say. . . . Mr. Brough was a clear-headed man.  She couldn't imagine how he stayed in the Church. . . . She hoped he hated that sickening, sickening, idiot humbug, Eve . . . meek . . . with silly long hair . . . "divinely smiling" . . . Adam was like a German . . . English too. . . . Impudent bombastic creature . . . a sort of man who would call his wife "my dear."  There was a hymn that even Pater liked . . . the tune was like a garden in the autumn. . . .

O . . . Strengthen *Stay*--up-- . . . Holding--all Cre--ay--ay--tion. . . . Who . . . ever Dost Thy . . . self--un . . . Moved--a--Bide. . . . Thyself unmoved abide . . . Thyself unmoved abide . . . Unmoved abide . . .

Unmoved abide. . . . Unmoved Abide . . .

. . . Flights of shining steps, shallow and very wide--going up and up and growing fainter and fainter, and far away at the top a faint old face with great rays shooting out all round it . . . the picture in the large "Pilgrim's Progress." . . . God in heaven. . . . I belong to Apollyon . . . a horror with expressionless eyes . . . darting out little spiky flames . . . if only it would come now . . . instead of waiting until the end. . . .

She clasped her hands closely one in the other.  They felt large and strong.  She stopped her thoughts and stared for a long while at the faint light in the room . . .

"It's physically impossible" someone had said . . . the only hell thinkable is remorse . . . remorse. . . .

Sighing impatiently she turned about . . . and sighed again, breathing deeply and rattling and feeling very hungry. . . . There will be breakfast, even for me. . . . If they knew me they would not give me breakfast. . . . no one would . . . I should be in a little room and one after another would come and be reproachful and shocked . . . and then they would go away and be happy and forget. . . .

Sarah would come. Whatever it was, Sarah would come. She read the Bible and marked pieces. . . . But she would rush in without saying anything, with a red face and bang down a plate of melon. . . . What did God do about people like Sarah? Perhaps Apollyon could be made to come at once--sweeping in like a large bat--be torn to bits--those men at that college said he had come to them. They swore--one after the other and the devil came in through one of the carved windows and carried one of them away. . . . I have my doubts . . . Pater's face laughing--I have my doubts, ooof--P-ooof. She flung off the outer covering and felt the strong movements of her limbs. Hang! Hang! *Hang!* DAMN. . . .

If there's no God, there's no Devil . . . and everything goes on. . . . Fraulein goes on having her school. . . . What does she really think? . . . Out in the world people don't think. . . . They grimace. . . . Is there anywhere where there are no people? . . . be a gipsy. . . . There are always people. . . .

8

"What a perfect morning . . . what a perfect morning," Miriam kept telling herself, trying to see into the garden. There was a bowl of irises on the breakfast-table--it made everything seem strange. There had never been flowers on the table before. There was also a great dish of pumpernickel besides the usual food. Fraulein had enjoined silence. The silence made the impression of the irises stay. She hoped it might be a new rule. She glanced at Fraulein two or three times. She was pallid white. Her face looked thinner than usual and her eyes larger and keener. She did not seem to notice anyone. Miriam wondered whether she were thinking about cancer. Her face looked as it had done when once or twice she had said, "Ich bin so bange vor Krebs." She hoped not. Perhaps it was the problem of evil. Perhaps she had thought of it when she put the irises on the table.

She gazed at them, half-feeling the flummery petals against the palm of her hand.  Fraulein seemed cancelled.  There was no need to feel self-conscious.  She was not thinking of any of them.  Miriam found herself looking at high grey stone basins with ornamental stems like wine-glasses and large square fluted pedestals, filled with geraniums and calceolarias.  They had stood in the sunshine at the corners of the lawn in her grandmother's garden.  She could remember nothing else but the scent of a greenhouse and its steamy panes over her head . . . lemon thyme and scented geranium.

How lovely it would be to-day at the end of the day.  Fraulein would feel happy then , . . or did elderly people fear cancer all the time. . . . It was a great mistake. You should leave things to Nature. . . . You were more likely to have things if you thought about them.  But Fraulein would think and worry . . . alone with herself . . . with her great dark eyes and bony forehead and thin pale cheeks . . . always alone, and just cancer coming . . . I shall be like that one day . . . an old teacher and cancer coming.  It was silly to forget all about it and see Granny's calceolarias in the sun . . . all that had to come to an end. . . . To forget was like putting off repentance.  Those who did not put it off saw when the great waters came, a shining figure coming to them through the flood. . . . If they did not they were like the man in a night-cap, his mouth hanging open--no teeth--and skinny hands, playing cards on his death-bed.

9

After bed-making, Fraulein settled a mending party at the window-end of the schoolroom table.  She sent no emissary but was waiting herself in the schoolroom when they came down.  She hovered about putting them into their places and en-quiring about the work of each one.

She arranged Miriam and the Germans at the saal end of the table for an Eng-lish lesson.  Mademoiselle was not there.  Fraulein herself took the head of the table.  Once more she enjoined silence--the whole table seemed waiting for Miriam to begin her lesson.

The three or four readings they had done during the term alone in the little room had brought them through about a third of the blue-bound volume. Hoarsely whispering, then violently clearing her throat and speaking suddenly in a very loud tone Miriam bade them resume the story. They read and she corrected them in hoarse whispers. No one appeared to be noticing. A steady breeze coming through the open door of the summer-house flowed past them and along the table, but Miriam sat stifling, with beating temples. She had no thoughts. Now and again in correcting a simple word she was not sure that she had given the right English rendering. Behind her distress two impressions went to and fro--Fraulein and the raccommodage party sitting in judgment and the whole roomful waiting for cancer.

Very gently at the end of half an hour Fraulein dismissed the Germans to practise.

Herr Schraub was coming at eleven. Miriam supposed she was free until then and went upstairs.

On the landing she met Mademoiselle coming downstairs with mending.

"Bossy coming?" she said feverishly in French; "are you going to the saal?"

Mademoiselle stood contemplating her.

"I've just been giving an English lesson, oh, Mon Dieu," she proceeded.

Mademoiselle still looked gravely and quietly.

Miriam was passing on. Mademoiselle turned and said hurriedly in a low voice. "Elsa says you are a fool at lessons."

"Oh," smiled Miriam.

"You think they do not speak of you, hein? Well, I tell you they speak of you. Jimmie says you are as fat as any German. She laughed in saying that. Gertrude, too, thinks you are a fool. Oh, they say things. If I should tell you all the things they say you would not believe."

"I dare say," said Miriam heavily, moving on.

"Everyone, all say things, I tell you," whispered Mademoiselle turning her head as she went on downstairs.

10

Miriam ran into the empty summer-house tearing open a well-filled envelope. There was a long letter from Eve, a folded half-sheet from mother. Her heart beat rapidly.  Thick straight rain was seething down into the garden.

"Come and say good-bye to Mademoiselle, Hendy."

"Is she *going?*"

"Umph."

"Little Mademoiselle?"

"Poor little beast!"

"Leaving!"

"Seems like it--she's been packing all the morning."

"Because of that letter business?"

"Oh, I dunno.  Anyhow there's some story of some friend of Fraulein's travelling through to Besan on today and Mademoiselle's going with her and we're all to take solemn leave and she's not coming back next term.  Come on."

Mademoiselle, radiantly rosy under her large black French hat, wearing her stockinette jacket and grey dress, was standing at the end of the schoolroom table-- the girls were all assembled and the door into the hall was open.

The housekeeper was laughing and shouting and imitating the puffing of a train.  Mademoiselle stood smiling beside her with downcast eyes.

Opposite them was Gertrude with thin white face, blue lips and hotly blazing eyes fixed on Mademoiselle.  She stood easily with her hands clasped behind her.

She must have an appalling headache thought Miriam.  Mademoiselle began shaking hands.

"I say, Mademoiselle," began Jimmie quietly and hurriedly in her lame French, as she took her hand.  "Have you got another place?"

"A place?"

"I mean what are you going to do next term, petite?"

"Next term?"

"We want to know about your plans."

"But I remain now with my parents till my marriage."

"Petite!!!  Fancy never telling us."

Exclamations clustered round from all over the room.

"Why should I tell?"

"We didn't even know you were engaged!"

"But of course.  Certainly I marry.  I know quite well who is to marry me."

The room was taking leave of Mademoiselle almost in silence. The English were standing together. Miriam heard their voices. "'Dieu, m'selle, 'dieu, m'selle," one after the other and saw hands and wrists move vigorously up and down. The Germans were commenting, "Ah, she is engaged--ah, what-- *en-gaged.* Ah, the rascal! Hor mal--"

Miriam dreaded her turn. Mademoiselle was coming near . . . so cheap and common-looking with her hard grey dress and her cheap jacket with the hat hiding her hair and making her look skinny and old. She was a more dreadful stranger than she had been at first . . . Miriam wished she could stay. She could not let anyone go away like this. They would not meet again and Mademoiselle was going away detesting her and them all, going away in disgrace and not minding and going to be married. All the time there had been that waiting for her. She was smiling now and showing her babyish teeth. How could Jimmie hold her by the shoulders?

"Venez mon enfant, venez a l'instant," called Fraulein from the hall.

Mademoiselle made her hard little sound with her throat.

"Why doesn't she go?" thought Miriam as Mademoiselle ran down the room. "Adieu, adieu evaireeboddie--alla----"

11

"Are all here?"

Jimmie answered and Fraulein came to the table and stood leaning for a moment upon one hand.

The door opened and the housekeeper shone hard and bright in the doorway.

"Wasche angekommen!"

"Na, gut," responded Fraulein quietly.

The housekeeper disappeared.

"Fraulein looks like a dead body," thought Miriam.

Apprehension overtook her . . . "there's going to be some silly fuss."

"I shall speak in English, because the most that I shall say concerns the English members of this household and its heavy seriousness will be by those who are not English, sufficiently understood."

Miriam flushed, struggling for self-possession. She determined not to listen.

. . . Damn . . . Devil . . ." she exhorted herself . . . "humbugging creature . . ." She felt the blood throbbing in her face and her eyes and looked at no one.  She was conscious that little movements and sounds came from the Germans, but she heard nothing but Fraulein's voice which had ceased.  It had been the clear-cut low-breathing tone she used at prayers.  "Oh, Lord, bother, damnation," she reiterated in her discomfiture.  The words echoing through her mind seemed to cut a way of escape. . . .

"That dear child," smiled Fraulein's voice, "who has just left us, came under this roof . . . nearly a year ago.

"She came, a tender girl (Mademoiselle--Mademoiselle, oh, goodness!) from the house of her pious parents, fromme Eltern, fromme Eltern."  Fraulein breathed these words slowly out and a deep sigh came from one of the Germans, "to reside with us.  She came in the most perfect confidence with the aim to complete her own simple education, the pious and simple nurture of a Protestant French girl, and with the aim also to remove for a period something of the burden lying upon the shoulders of those dear parents in the upbringing of herself and her brothers and sisters" (And then to leave home and be married--how easy, how easy!)

"Honourably--honourably she has fulfilled each and every duty laid upon her as institutrice in this establishment.

"Sufficient to indicate this fulfilment of duty is the fact that she was happy and that she made happy others----"

Fraulein's voice dropped to its lowest note and grew fuller in tone.

"Would that I could here complete what I have to say of the sojourn of little Aline Ducorroy under this roof. . . . But that I cannot do.

"That I cannot do.

"It has been the experience of this pure and gentle soul to come, under this roof, in contact with things not pure."

Fraulein's voice had become breathless and shaking.  Both her hands sought the support of the table.

"This poor child has had unwillingly to suffer the fact of associating with those not pure."

"Ach, Fraulein!  What you say!" ejaculated Clara.

In the silence the leaves of the chestnut tree tapped one against the other.

Miriam listened to them . . . there must be a little breeze blowing across the garden. Why had she not noticed it before? Were they all hearing it?

"With--those--not pure."

"Here, in this my school."

Miriam's heart began to beat angrily.

"She has been forced, here, in this school, to hear talking"--Fraulein's voice thickened--"of men . . . ."

*"Manner--geschichten . . . here!"*

*"Manner--geschichten."* Fraulein's voice rang out down the table. She bent forward so that the light from both the windows behind her fell sharply across her grey-clad shoulders and along the top of her head. There was no condemnation Miriam felt in those broad grey shoulders--they were innocent. But the head shining and flat, the wide parting, the sleekness of the hair falling thinly and flatly away from it--angry, dreadful skull. She writhed away from it. She would not look any more. She felt her neck was swelling her collar-band.

Fraulein whispered low.

"Here in my school, here standing round this table are those who talk of--men.

"Young girls . . . who talk . . . of men."

While Fraulein waited, trembling, several of the girls began to snuffle and sob.

"Is there, can there be in the world anything that is more base, more vile, more impure? Is there? Is there?"

Miriam wished she knew who was crying. She tried to fix her thoughts on a hole in the table-cover. "It could be darned. . . . It could he darned."

"You are brought here together, each and all of you here together in the time of your youth. It is, it should be for you the most beautiful occasion. Can you find anything more terrible than that such occasion where all may work and influence each other--for all life--in purity and goodness--that such occasion should he used--impurely? Like a dawn, like a dawn for purity should be the life of a maiden. Calm, and pure and with holy prayer."

Miriam repeated these words in her mind trying to dwell on the beauty of Fraulein's middle tones. "And the day shall come, I shall wish, for all of you, that the sanctity of a home shall be within your hands.  What then shall be the shame, what the regret of those who before the coming of that sacred time did think thoughts of men, did speak of them?  ***Shame, shame,***" whispered Fraulein amidst the sobbing girls.

"With the thoughts of those who have this impure nature I can do nothing. For them it is freely to acknowledge this evil in the heart and to pray that the heart may be changed and made clean.

"But a thing I can do and I do. . . . I will have no more of this talking.  In my school I will have no more. . . . Do you hear, all?  Do you hear?"

She struck the table with both fists and brandished them in mid-air.

"Eh-h," she sneered.  "I know, *I* know who are the culprits.  I have always known."  She gasped.  "It shall cease--these talks--this vile talk of men.  Do you understand?  It shall cease.  I--will--not--have it. . . . The school shall be clean . . . from pupil to pupil . . . from room to room. . . . Every day . . . every hour. . . . Shameless!" she screamed.  "Shameless.  Ah!  I know.  I know you."  She stood with her arms folded, swaying, and gave a little laugh.  "You think to deceive me.  You do not deceive me.  I know.  I have known and I shall know.  This school is mine. Mine!  My place!  I will have it as I will have it.  That is clear and plain, and you all shall help me.  I shall say no more.  But I shall know what to do."

Mechanically Miriam went downstairs with the rest of the party.  With the full force of her nerves she resisted the echoes of Fraulein's onslaught, refusing to think of anything she had said and blotting out her image every time it rose.  The essential was that she would be dismissed as Mademoiselle had been dismissed.  That was the upshot of it all for her.  Fraulein was a mad, silly, pious female who would send her away and go on glowering over the Bible.  She would have to go, go, *go* in a sort of disgrace.

The girls were talking all round her, excitedly.  She despised them for showing that they were disturbed by Fraulein's despotic nonsense.  As they reached the basement she remembered the letter crushed in her hand and sat down on the last step to glance through it.

## 12

"Dearest Mim. I have a wonderful piece of news for you. I wonder what you will say? It is about Harriett. She has asked me to tell you as she does not like to write about it herself."

With steady hands Miriam turned the closely-written sheets reading a phrase here and there . . . "regularly in the seat behind us at All Saints' for months--saw her with the Pooles at a concert at the Assembly Rooms and made up his mind then-- the moment he saw her--joined the tennis-club--they won the double handicap--a beautiful Slazenger racquet--only just over sixteen--for years--of course Mother says it's just a little foolish nonsense--but I am not sure that she really thinks so-- Gerald took me into his confidence--made a solemn call-- *admirably* suited to each other--rather a long melancholy good-looking face--they look such a contrast--the big Canadian Railway--not exactly a clerk--something rather above that, to do with making drafts of things and so on. Very sweet and charming--my own young days- -that I have reached the great age of twenty-three--resident post in the country-- two little girls--we think it very good pay--I shall go in September--plenty of time- -that you should come home for the long holidays. We are all looking forward to it--the tennis-club--your name as a holiday member--the American tournament in August--Harry was the youngest lady member like you--of course Harry could not let you come without knowing--find somebody travelling through--Fraulein Pfaff- -expect to see you looking like a flour-sack with a string tied round its waist--all the dwarf roses in bloom--hardly any strawberries--we shall see you soon--everybody sends."

Miriam got up and swung the half-read letter above her head like a dumb-bell.

She looked about her like a stranger--everything was as it had been the day she came--the little cramped basement hall--the strange German girls--small and old looking, poking about amongst the baskets. She hardly knew them. She passed half-blindly amongst them with her eyes wide. The little dressing-room seemed full of bright light. She saw everyone at once clearly. All the English girls were there. She knew every line of each of them. They were her old friends. They knew her. Looking at none of them she felt she embraced them all, closely, and that they knew it. They shone. They were beautiful. She wanted to cry aloud. She was English and free. She had nothing to do with this German school. Baskets at her feet made her pick her way. Solomon was kneeling at one, sorting and handing out. At a little table under the window Millie stood jotting pencil notes on a pocket-book. Judy was at her side. The others were grouped about the piano. Gertrude sat on the keyboard her legs dangling.

Miriam plumped down on a full basket.

"Hullo, Hendy, old chap, *you* look all right!"

Miriam looked fearlessly up at the faces that were turned towards her. Again she seemed to see all of them at once. The circle of her vision seemed huge. It was as if the confining rim of her glasses were gone and she saw equally from eyes that seemed to fill her face. She drew all their eyes to her. They were waiting for her to speak. For a moment it seemed as if they stood there lifeless. She had drawn all their meaning and all their happiness into herself. She could do as she wished with them--their poor little lives.

They stood waiting for some word from her. She dropped her eyes and caught the flash of Gertrude's swinging steel buckles.

"Wasn't Fraulein angry?" she said carelessly.

Someone pushed the door to.

"Sly old bird."

"Fancy imagining we shouldn't see through Mademoiselle leaving."

"H'm," said Miriam.

"I knew Mademoiselle *would* sneak if she had half a chance."

"Yes, ever since she got so thick with Elsa."

"Oh!--Elsa."

"You bet Fraulein looks down on the two of them in her heart of hearts."

"M'm--she's fairly sick, Jemima, with the lot of us this time."

"Mademoiselle told her some pretty things," laughed Gertrude. "Lily thinks we're lost souls--nearly all of us."

"Onny swaw, my dears, onny swaw."

"It's all very well. But there's no knowing what Mademoiselle would make her believe. She'd got reams about you, Hendy--nothing bad enough."

"H'm," said Miriam, "I can imagine----"

Her thoughts brought back a day when she had shown Mademoiselle the names in her birthday-book and dwelt on one page and let Mademoiselle understand that it was the page--brown eyes--les yeux brunes foncees. Why did Mademoiselle and Fraulein think that bad--want to spoil it for her? She had said nothing about the confidences of the German girls to anyone. Elsa must have found that out from Clara.

"Oh, well it's all over now. Let's be thankful and think no more about it."

"All very fine, Jemima. You're going home."

"Thank goodness."

"And not coming back. Lucky Pigleinchen."

"Well, so am I," said Miriam, "and I'm not coming back."

"I say! Aren't you coming to Norderney?" Gertrude flashed dark eyes at her.

"Can't you come to Norderney?" said Judy thickly, at her elbow.

"Well, you see there are all sorts of things happening at home. I must go. One of my sisters is engaged and another going away. I *must* go home for a while. Of course I *might* come back."

"Think it over, Henderson, and see if you can't decide in our favour."

"We shall have another Miss Owen."

Miriam struggled up out of her basket. "But I thought you all *liked* Miss Owen!"

"Ho! Goodness! Too simple for words."

"You never told us you had any sisters, Hendy," said Jimmie, tapping her on the wrist.

"What a pity you're going just as we're getting to know you," Judy smiled shyly and looked on the floor.

"Well--I'm off with my bundle," announced Gertrude. "To be continued in our next. Think it over, Hendy. Don't desert us. Hurry up, my room. It'll be tea-time before we're straight. Come on, Jim."

Miriam moved, with Judy following at her elbow, across the room to Millie. She looked up with her little plaintive frown. Miriam could not remember what her plans were. "Let's see," she said, "you're going to Norderney, aren't you?"

"I'm not going to Norderney," said Nellie almost tearfully. "I only wish I were.

I don't even know I'm coming back next term."

"Aren't you looking forward to the holidays?"

"I don't know. I'd rather be staying here if I'm not coming back after."

"To stay in Germany? You'd rather do that than anything?"

"Rather."

"Here, with Fraulein Pfaff?"

"Of course, here with Fraulein Pfaff. I'd rather be in Germany than any-thing."

Millie stood staring with her pout and her slightly raised eyebrows at the frost-ed window.

"Would you stay here in the school for the holidays if Fraulein were staying?"

"I'd do anything," said Millie, "to stay in Germany."

"You know," said Miriam gazing at her, "so would I--any mortal thing."

Millie's eyes had filled with tears.

"Then why don't ye stay?" said Judy, with gentle gruffness.

13

The house was shut up for the night.

Miriam looked up at the clock dizzily as she drank the last of her coffee. It marked half-past eleven. Fraulein had told her to be ready at a quarter to twelve. Her hands felt large and shaky and her feet were cold. The room was stifling--bare and brown in the gaslight. She left it and crept through the hall where her trunk stood and up the creaking stairs. She turned up the gas. Emma lay asleep with red eyelids and cheeks. Miriam did not look at Ulrica. Hurriedly and desolately she packed her bag. She was going home empty-handed. She had achieved nothing. Fraulein had made not the slightest effort to keep her. She was just nothing again--with her Saratoga trunk and her hand-bag. Harriett had achieved. Harriett. She was just going home with nothing to say for herself.

"The carriage is here, my child. Make haste."

Miriam pushed things hurriedly into her bag. Fraulein had gone downstairs.

She was ready. She looked numbly round the room. Emma looked very far away. She turned out the gas. The dim light from the landing shone into the room.

She stood for a moment in the doorway looking back. The room seemed to be empty. There seemed to be nothing in it but the black screen standing round the bed that was no longer hers.

"Good-bye," she murmured and hurried downstairs.

In the hall Fraulein began to talk at once, talking until they were seated side by side in the dark cab.

Then Miriam gazed freely at the pale profile shining at her side. Poor Fraulein Pfaff, getting old.

Fraulein began to ask about Miriam's plans for the future. Miriam answered as to an equal, elaborating a little account of circumstances at home, and the doings of her sisters. As she spoke she felt that Fraulein envied her her youth and her family at home in England--and she raised her voice a little and laughed easily and moved, crossing her knees in the cab.

She used sentimental German words about Harriett--a description of her that might have applied to Emma--little emphatic tender epithets came to her from the conversations of the girls. Fraulein praised her German warmly and asked question after question about the house and garden at Barnes and presently of her mother.

"I can't talk about her," said Miriam shortly.

"That is English," murmured Fraulein.

"She's such a little thing," said Miriam, "smaller than any of us." Presently Fraulein laid her gloved hand on Miriam's gloved one. "You and I have, I think, much in common."

Miriam froze--and looked at the gas-lamps slowly swinging by along the boulevard. "Much will have happened in England whilst you have been here with us," said Fraulein eagerly.

They reached a street--shuttered darkness where the shops were, and here and there the yellow flare of a cafe. She strained her eyes to see the faces and forms of men and women--breathing more quickly as she watched the characteristic German gait.

There was the station.

Her trunk was weighed and registered. There was something to pay. She handed her purse to Fraulein and stood gazing at the uniformed man--ruddy and clear-eyed--clear hard blue eyes and hard clean clear yellow moustaches--decisive untroubled movements.  Passengers were walking briskly about and laughing and shouting remarks to each other.  The train stood waiting for her.  The ringing of an enormous bell brought her hands to her ears.  Fraulein gently propelled her up the three steps into a compartment marked Damen--Coupe.  It smelt of biscuits and wine.

A man with a booming voice came to examine her ticket.  He stood bending under the central light, uttering sturdy German words.  Miriam drank them in without understanding.  He left the carriage very empty.  The great bell was ringing again.  Fraulein standing on the top step pressed both her hands and murmured words of farewell.

"Leb' wohl, mein Kind, Gott segne dich."

"Good-bye, Fraulein," she said stiffly, shaking hands.

The door was shut with a slam--the light seemed to go down.  Miriam glanced at it--half the dull green muslin shade had slipped over the gas-globe.  The carriage seemed dark.  The platform outside was very bright.  Fraulein had disappeared.  The train was high above the platform.  Politely smiling Miriam scrambled to the window.  The platform was moving, the large bright station moving away.  Fraulein's wide smile was creasing and caverning under her hat from which the veil was thrown back.

Standing at the window Miriam smiled sharply.  Fraulein's form flowed slowly away with the platform.

Groups passed by smiling and waving.

Miriam sat down.

She leaped up to lean from the window.

The platform had disappeared.

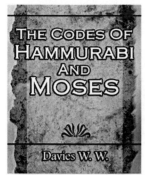

### The Codes Of Hammurabi And Moses
### W. W. Davies

QTY

The discovery of the Hammurabi Code is one of the greatest achievements of archaeology, and is of paramount interest, not only to the student of the Bible, but also to all those interested in ancient history...

**Religion**     ISBN: *1-59462-338-4*          Pages:132
*MSRP $12.95*

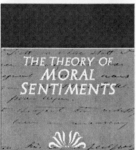

### The Theory of Moral Sentiments
### Adam Smith

QTY

This work from 1749. contains original theories of conscience amd moral judgment and it is the foundation for systemof morals.

**Philosophy**  ISBN: *1-59462-777-0*          Pages:536
*MSRP $19.95*

### Jessica's First Prayer
### Hesba Stretton

QTY

In a screened and secluded corner of one of the many railway-bridges which span the streets of London there could be seen a few years ago, from five o'clock every morning until half past eight, a tidily set-out coffee-stall, consisting of a trestle and board, upon which stood two large tin cans, with a small fire of charcoal burning under each so as to keep the coffee boiling during the early hours of the morning when the work-people were thronging into the city on their way to their daily toil...

Pages:84

**Childrens**  ISBN: *1-59462-373-2*          *MSRP $9.95*

### My Life and Work
### Henry Ford

QTY

Henry Ford revolutionized the world with his implementation of mass production for the Model T automobile. Gain valuable business insight into his life and work with his own auto-biography... "We have only started on our development of our country we have not as yet, with all our talk of wonderful progress, done more than scratch the surface. The progress has been wonderful enough but..."

Pages:300

**Biographies/**     ISBN: *1-59462-198-5*          *MSRP $21.95*

www.bookjungle.com *email: sales@bookjungle.com fax: 630-214-0564 mail: Book Jungle PO Box 2226 Champaign, IL 61825*

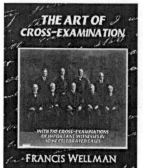

## The Art of Cross-Examination
## Francis Wellman

QTY

I presume it is the experience of every author, after his first book is published upon an important subject, to be almost overwhelmed with a wealth of ideas and illustrations which could readily have been included in his book, and which to his own mind, at least, seem to make a second edition inevitable. Such certainly was the case with me; and when the first edition had reached its sixth impression in five months, I rejoiced to learn that it seemed to my publishers that the book had met with a sufficiently favorable reception to justify a second and considerably enlarged edition. ...

**Pages:412**

Reference    ISBN: *1-59462-647-2*    *MSRP $19.95*

## On the Duty of Civil Disobedience
## Henry David Thoreau

QTY

Thoreau wrote his famous essay, On the Duty of Civil Disobedience, as a protest against an unjust but popular war and the immoral but popular institution of slave-owning. He did more than write—he declined to pay his taxes, and was hauled off to gaol in consequence. Who can say how much this refusal of his hastened the end of the war and of slavery?

Law    ISBN: *1-59462-747-9*    **Pages:48**

*MSRP $7.45*

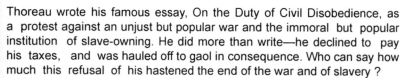

## Dream Psychology Psychoanalysis for Beginners
## Sigmund Freud

QTY

Sigmund Freud, born Sigismund Schlomo Freud (May 6, 1856 - September 23, 1939), was a Jewish-Austrian neurologist and psychiatrist who co-founded the psychoanalytic school of psychology. Freud is best known for his theories of the unconscious mind, especially involving the mechanism of repression; his redefinition of sexual desire as mobile and directed towards a wide variety of objects; and his therapeutic techniques, especially his understanding of transference in the therapeutic relationship and the presumed value of dreams as sources of insight into unconscious desires.

**Pages:196**

Psychology    ISBN: *1-59462-905-6*    *MSRP $15.45*

## The Miracle of Right Thought
## Orison Swett Marden

QTY

Believe with all of your heart that you will do what you were made to do. When the mind has once formed the habit of holding cheerful, happy, prosperous pictures, it will not be easy to form the opposite habit. It does not matter how improbable or how far away this realization may see, or how dark the prospects may be, if we visualize them as best we can, as vividly as possible, hold tenaciously to them and vigorously struggle to attain them, they will gradually become actualized, realized in the life. But a desire, a longing without endeavor, a yearning abandoned or held indifferently will vanish without realization.

**Pages:360**

Self Help    ISBN: *1-59462-644-8*    *MSRP $25.45*

**The Rosicrucian Cosmo-Conception Mystic Christianity** *by Max Heindel*     ISBN: *1-59462-188-8*   **$38.95**
*The Rosicrucian Cosmo-conception is not dogmatic, neither does it appeal to any other authority than the reason of the student. It is: not controversial, but is: sent forth in the, hope that it may help to clear...*     *New Age/Religion Pages 646*

**Abandonment To Divine Providence** *by Jean-Pierre de Caussade*     ISBN: *1-59462-228-0*   **$25.95**
*"The Rev. Jean Pierre de Caussade was one of the most remarkable spiritual writers of the Society of Jesus in France in the 18th Century. His death took place at Toulouse in 1751. His works have gone through many editions and have been republished...*     *Inspirational Religion Pages 400*

**Mental Chemistry** *by Charles Haanel*     ISBN: *1-59462-192-6*   **$23.95**
*Mental Chemistry allows the change of material conditions by combining and appropriately utilizing the power of the mind. Much like applied chemistry creates something new and unique out of careful combinations of chemicals the mastery of mental chemistry...*     *New Age Pages 354*

**The Letters of Robert Browning and Elizabeth Barret Barrett 1845-1846 vol II**     ISBN: *1-59462-193-4*   **$35.95**
*by Robert Browning and Elizabeth Barrett*     *Biographies Pages 596*

**Gleanings In Genesis (volume I)** *by Arthur W. Pink*     ISBN: *1-59462-130-6*   **$27.45**
*Appropriately has Genesis been termed "the seed plot of the Bible" for in it we have, in germ form, almost all of the great doctrines which are afterwards fully developed in the books of Scripture which follow...*     *Religion/Inspirational Pages 420*

**The Master Key** *by L. W. de Laurence*     ISBN: *1-59462-001-6*   **$30.95**
*In no branch of human knowledge has there been a more lively increase of the spirit of research during the past few years than in the study of Psychology, Concentration and Mental Discipline. The requests for authentic lessons in Thought Control, Mental Discipline and...*     *New Age/Business Pages 422*

**The Lesser Key Of Solomon Goetia** *by L. W. de Laurence*     ISBN: *1-59462-092-X*   **$9.95**
*This translation of the first book of the "Lemegton" which is now for the first time made accessible to students of Talismanic Magic was done, after careful collation and edition, from numerous Ancient Manuscripts in Hebrew, Latin, and French...*     *New Age/Occult Pages 92*

**Rubaiyat Of Omar Khayyam** *by Edward Fitzgerald*     ISBN:*1-59462-332-5*   **$13.95**
*Edward Fitzgerald, whom the world has already learned, in spite of his own efforts to remain within the shadow of anonymity, to look upon as one of the rarest poets of the century, was born at Bredfield, in Suffolk, on the 31st of March, 1809. He was the third son of John Purcell...*     *Music Pages 172*

**Ancient Law** *by Henry Maine*     ISBN: *1-59462-128-4*   **$29.95**
*The chief object of the following pages is to indicate some of the earliest ideas of mankind, as they are reflected in Ancient Law, and to point out the relation of those ideas to modern thought.*     *Religion/History Pages 452*

**Far-Away Stories** *by William J. Locke*     ISBN: *1-59462-129-2*   **$19.45**
*"Good wine needs no bush, but a collection of mixed vintages does. And this book is just such a collection. Some of the stories I do not want to remain buried for ever in the museum files of dead magazine-numbers an author's not unpardonable vanity..."*     *Fiction Pages 272*

**Life of David Crockett** *by David Crockett*     ISBN: *1-59462-250-7*   **$27.45**
*"Colonel David Crockett was one of the most remarkable men of the times in which he lived. Born in humble life, but gifted with a strong will, an indomitable courage, and unremitting perseverance...*     *Biographies/New Age Pages 424*

**Lip-Reading** *by Edward Nitchie*     ISBN: *1-59462-206-X*   **$25.95**
*Edward B. Nitchie, founder of the New York School for the Hard of Hearing, now the Nitchie School of Lip-Reading, Inc, wrote "LIP-READING Principles and Practice". The development and perfecting of this meritorious work on lip-reading was an undertaking...*     *How-to Pages 400*

**A Handbook of Suggestive Therapeutics, Applied Hypnotism, Psychic Science**     ISBN: *1-59462-214-0*   **$24.95**
*by Henry Munro*     *Health/New Age/Health/Self-help Pages 376*

**A Doll's House: and Two Other Plays** *by Henrik Ibsen*     ISBN: *1-59462-112-8*   **$19.95**
*Henrik Ibsen created this classic when in revolutionary 1848 Rome. Introducing some striking concepts in playwriting for the realist genre, this play has been studied the world over.*     *Fiction/Classics/Plays 308*

**The Light of Asia** *by sir Edwin Arnold*     ISBN: *1-59462-204-3*   **$13.95**
*In this poetic masterpiece, Edwin Arnold describes the life and teachings of Buddha. The man who was to become known as Buddha to the world was born as Prince Gautama of India but he rejected the worldly riches and abandoned the reigns of power when...*     *Religion/History/Biographies Pages 170*

**The Complete Works of Guy de Maupassant** *by Guy de Maupassant*     ISBN: *1-59462-157-8*   **$16.95**
*"For days and days, nights and nights, I had dreamed of that first kiss which was to consecrate our engagement, and I knew not on what spot I should put my lips..."*     *Fiction/Classics Pages 240*

**The Art of Cross-Examination** *by Francis L. Wellman*     ISBN: *1-59462-309-0*   **$26.95**
*Written by a renowned trial lawyer, Wellman imparts his experience and uses case studies to explain how to use psychology to extract desired information through questioning.*     *How-to/Science/Reference Pages 408*

**Answered or Unanswered?** *by Louisa Vaughan*     ISBN: *1-59462-248-5*   **$10.95**
*Miracles of Faith in China*     *Religion Pages 112*

**The Edinburgh Lectures on Mental Science (1909)** *by Thomas*     ISBN: *1-59462-008-3*   **$11.95**
*This book contains the substance of a course of lectures recently given by the writer in the Queen Street Hall, Edinburgh. Its purpose is to indicate the Natural Principles governing the relation between Mental Action and Material Conditions...*     *New Age/Psychology Pages 148*

**Ayesha** *by H. Rider Haggard*     ISBN: *1-59462-301-5*   **$24.95**
*Verily and indeed it is the unexpected that happens! Probably if there was one person upon the earth from whom the Editor of this, and of a certain previous history, did not expect to hear again...*     *Classics Pages 380*

**Ayala's Angel** *by Anthony Trollope*     ISBN: *1-59462-352-X*   **$29.95**
*The two girls were both pretty, but Lucy who was twenty-one who supposed to be simple and comparatively unattractive, whereas Ayala was credited, as her Bombwhat romantic name might show, with poetic charm and a taste for romance. Ayala when her father died was nineteen...*     *Fiction Pages 484*

**The American Commonwealth** *by James Bryce*     ISBN: *1-59462-286-8*   **$34.45**
*An interpretation of American democratic political theory. It examines political mechanics and society from the perspective of Scotsman James Bryce*     *Politics Pages 572*

**Stories of the Pilgrims** *by Margaret P. Pumphrey*     ISBN: *1-59462-116-0*   **$17.95**
*This book explores pilgrims religious oppression in England as well as their escape to Holland and eventual crossing to America on the Mayflower, and their early days in New England...*     *History Pages 268*

**QTY**

**The Fasting Cure** *by Sinclair Upton*                    ISBN: *1-59462-222-1*  **$13.95**
*In the Cosmopolitan Magazine for May, 1910, and in the Contemporary Review (London) for April, 1910, I published an article dealing with my experiences in fasting. I have written a great many magazine articles, but never one which attracted so much attention...  New Age/Self Help/Health Pages 164*

**Hebrew Astrology** *by Sepharial*                         ISBN: *1-59462-308-2*  **$13.45**
*In these days of advanced thinking it is a matter of common observation that we have left many of the old landmarks behind and that we are now pressing forward to greater heights and to a wider horizon than that which represented the mind-content of our progenitors...  Astrology Pages 144*

**Thought Vibration or The Law of Attraction in the Thought World**   ISBN: *1-59462-127-6*  **$12.95**
*by William Walker Atkinson*                                *Psychology/Religion Pages 144*

**Optimism** *by Helen Keller*                              ISBN: *1-59462-108-X*  **$15.95**
*Helen Keller was blind, deaf, and mute since 19 months old, yet famously learned how to overcome these handicaps, communicate with the world, and spread her lectures promoting optimism.  An inspiring read for everyone...  Biographies/Inspirational Pages 84*

**Sara Crewe** *by Frances Burnett*                         ISBN: *1-59462-360-0*  **$9.45**
*In the first place, Miss Minchin lived in London. Her home was a large, dull, tall one, in a large, dull square, where all the houses were alike, and all the sparrows were alike, and where all the door-knockers made the same heavy sound...  Childrens Classic Pages 88*

**The Autobiography of Benjamin Franklin** *by Benjamin Franklin*   ISBN: *1-59462-135-7*  **$24.95**
*The Autobiography of Benjamin Franklin has probably been more extensively read than any other American historical work, and no other book of its kind has had such ups and downs of fortune. Franklin lived for many years in England, where he was agent...  Biographies/History Pages 332*

| Name | |
|---|---|
| Email | |
| Telephone | |
| Address | |
| | |
| City, State ZIP | |

☐ **Credit Card**          ☐ **Check / Money Order**

| Credit Card Number | |
|---|---|
| Expiration Date | |
| Signature | |

Please Mail to:  Book Jungle
                 PO Box 2226
                 Champaign, IL 61825
or Fax to:       630-214-0564

## ORDERING INFORMATION

**web**: *www.bookjungle.com*
**email**: *sales@bookjungle.com*
**fax**: *630-214-0564*
**mail**: *Book Jungle  PO Box 2226  Champaign, IL 61825*
**or PayPal** *to sales@bookjungle.com*

*Please contact us for bulk discounts*

## DIRECT-ORDER TERMS

**20% Discount if You Order
Two or More Books**
Free Domestic Shipping!
Accepted: Master Card, Visa,
Discover, American Express

CPSIA information can be obtained at www.ICGtesting.com
Printed in the USA
BVOW040641110113

310238BV00004B/56/P